There Must Be Horses

There Must Be Horses

Diana Kimpton

Diana Kimpton

First published as a Kindle ebook in 2012
Print edition published in 2012
Reprinted in 2013

Published by Diana Kimpton
25 Solent View Road, Cowes,
Isle of Wight, PO31 8JY
United Kingdom

www.dianakimpton.co.uk

Cover pictures from www.istockphoto.com

ISBN 978-0-9573414-2-5

Chapter 1

Sasha was determined not to cry. She hadn't when she'd left any of the other places, and she didn't want to break that record now. So she kept her head high and stared straight ahead through the windscreen.

Fran switched on the engine and put the car into gear. "Don't you want to wave goodbye?" she asked.

Sasha shook her head and scowled. Trust a social worker to make a stupid suggestion like that. Didn't she realise there was no point in looking back? This part of her life was over, just like all the placements before it. If that lot didn't want her any more, she didn't want them either.

"How are you feeling?" asked Fran, as she drove out of the drive and turned right towards the main road.

Sasha ignored her. She was too busy trying to catch one last glimpse of the Shetland pony in the field opposite. He was close to the fence, as usual, and he pricked his ears forward as they drove past. Did he realise this was the last time she would ever see him?

She turned her head and watched him disappear into the distance. Talking to that pony had been one of the few good things about her stay with Georgina and Gerald. The others were the riding lessons, of course, but they stopped as soon as Cynthia fell off.

"I asked how you're feeling," said Fran.

Sasha rolled her eyes upward and sighed. Why were social workers so irritating? She'd lost count of how many she'd had since she first came into care. They bounded into her life, made out they were her best friend and then left again with barely a goodbye. Fran was the latest and, like all the others, she thought she had the right to know everything. But Sasha had only known her a month and had no intention of revealing her innermost secrets.

"I'm fine," she lied, still staring out of the side window. She hoped she'd spot some more horses, but she didn't. As the car sped along the main road and onto the motorway, the only animals she saw in the fields were cows and sheep.

They'd been driving for half an hour when Fran pulled into a motorway service station and parked. "Time for tea," she said as she turned off the engine.

Sasha's stomach told her this was a good idea, but her heart wasn't so sure. Everything she owned was in her rucksack and the black plastic sacks that filled the back of the car. She didn't want to risk losing any of them. "Can't we keep going? I'm sure they'll find me something to eat at the home, even if I've missed supper."

Fran shook her head. "I need a break from driving," she explained. "And we need a little talk. Your stuff will be fine here – I'll lock the car, I promise."

The last comment took Sasha by surprise. She hadn't expected Fran to be so tuned into how she was feeling. But she still didn't trust her – too many social workers had broken promises before, especially ones of the "It'll be fine" variety. So she refused to walk away from the car until she'd tested the doors herself to make sure no one could get in. And she took her rucksack with her – her riding hat and her photos of her mum were too important to risk losing.

As they headed towards the main building, the setting sun painted pink edges on the dark clouds rolling in from the west. No wonder Sasha felt hungry. It was hours since lunch, and she hadn't had much of that anyway. Her mouth had been too dry with anxiety to eat the cheese sandwich that Georgina, mother of the dreaded Cynthia, had given her alone in her room.

The inside of the service station was bright and cheerful in a plastic sort of way. It was also very busy. The queue in the food hall was long and slow-moving. Sasha still didn't fancy talking so she turned her back on Fran and stared out across the crowded tables. To her relief, the social worker took the hint and didn't say anything while they waited for their turn.

Eventually the weary girl behind the counter asked, "Can I help you?" A badge on her uniform announced that her name was Mavis.

"Two burgers and fries, please," said Fran.

"No!" snapped Sasha. "I hate burgers." That wasn't strictly true, but she already had too little control over her own life. She didn't want a social worker deciding what she ate as well.

Fran sighed. "What do you want instead?" she asked.

Sasha scanned the pictures of food on the wall. This was Fran's treat so she chose the most expensive and unusual meal she could see – goat's cheese something or other with some weird-looking vegetables.

"Absolutely not," said Fran. "It's a burger or a baguette or nothing. The choice is yours."

Sasha was tempted to pick nothing in a fit of temper. But her stomach stopped her just in time, and she settled for an egg and tomato baguette.

Mavis piled their order on a tray and pushed it across the counter. "Have a nice day," she said.

Some chance, thought Sasha as she carried the food to the only empty table she could see. This wasn't the worse day of her life, but it was definitely a close runner-up. And there was still Fran's little talk to come. Judging by her previous experience of social workers, Sasha suspected that wasn't likely to make things better.

She was right. After they'd eaten in silence for a while, Fran dropped the bombshell. "The home can't have you back. They're full."

Sasha stared at her, open-mouthed in shock. She'd lived at Mountback Children's Home for almost a year before she moved to Cynthia's. Now the adoption wasn't going to happen, she'd automatically assumed she'd be going back. "You're wrong. They've got to have room."

"I'm sorry. They haven't." Fran reached forward to give Sasha's hand a sympathetic pat.

Sasha shifted her arm out of the way so fast that the tomato fell out of the remains of her baguette. She didn't bother to pick it up. She had more important things to think about. "I'm not very big. I could sleep in the bath, or they could put a camp bed in the office."

"That's not possible," said Fran. She spoke slowly, emphasising each word to get her point across. "Believe me. I'd have taken you there if I could. It would have been much easier than trying to find an emergency placement for you on a Saturday."

Sasha's heart sank to the bottom of her trainers as she realised she wasn't going back to people she knew. She'd got to start again with strangers. "So where am I going to live?" she asked, hardly daring to listen to the reply.

"I've found a nice place," said Fran. "I'm sure you'll like it."

The false brightness in her voice made Sasha suspicious. She stared at the social worker through narrowed eyes and asked, "What's wrong with it?"

"Nothing much. It's just temporary, that's all." Fran pushed away the remains of her meal and sat back in her chair. "Joe and Beth Turner weren't planning to foster anyone right now. But they've agreed to have you for a little while – just until we can find you somewhere else."

"Great," said Sasha with as much sarcasm as she could muster. "So you're dumping me with people who don't want me."

Fran sighed. "It's not that bad really. They're a lovely couple. I'm sure they'll make you welcome. And they were the best I could come up with at such short notice."

Sasha knew there was no point in arguing. Foster carers were thin on the ground, especially for twelve year olds. Georgina and Gerald had been the only people in the whole country who replied to the last "Sasha wants a home" advert.

But that didn't mean she liked what was happening. Moving in with strangers was always hard. But it was even worse when she knew she'd have to do it all over again soon.

She gulped down the last of her baguette, climbed wearily to her feet and swung her rucksack on her back. "Let's go," she said. The sooner this journey was over, the sooner she'd find out what fate and Social Services had in store for her this time.

"Okay," said Fran, with a look of relief. She stood up and led the way outside into the semi-darkness.

Sasha grabbed the social worker's unfinished bag of fries from the table and munched its contents on the way to the car. There was no point in wasting good food, especially when she had no idea what would be on offer at the next place.

Fran walked back to the car in silence. It was only as she checked Sasha had done her seat belt up properly that she spoke again. "I hope you're going to behave this time."

"Me!" said Sasha, with faked innocence. "When did I ever not behave?"

"This morning! You'd still be at Georgina and Gerald's if you hadn't smashed all Cynthia's ornaments."

Sasha bristled with indignation. "She's lying. I didn't break them all." Even in the enormity of her rage, she'd left the china horse untouched.

"The exact details don't matter," said Fran. "What you did was wrong."

"And what she said was mean," added Sasha, with a scowl.

"Which was?"

"That's none of your business." Sasha folded her arms defiantly and turned away. She didn't want anyone else to know what Cynthia had said. Suppose they thought the same. Suppose it was true.

Chapter 2

It started to rain as they drove back onto the motorway, adding a gloominess to the journey that matched Sasha's mood. Fran seemed more cheerful. "Shall I tell you about Joe and Beth while I drive," she suggested, above the annoying squeak of the windscreen wipers.

"No!" said Sasha. What was the point if she wasn't going to be with them for long? The safe plan would be to spend most of her time in her room so she didn't get to know them much at all. The less she put down roots, the less it would hurt to leave.

To avoid any more attempts at conversation, she huddled down in the front seat and pretended to doze. She did it so effectively that she was soon fast asleep, lulled by the swish of the tyres on the wet road and the steady rhythm of the engine.

The next thing she knew was Fran tapping her on the shoulder. "Wake up! We're here."

Sasha opened her eyes to almost total darkness. That was a surprise. Why weren't the street lights on? She opened the car door and was relieved to see the interior lamp switch on. But its dim glow wasn't bright enough to let her see where she was.

The rain had stopped and the night air carried the hint of a smell she almost recognised. But there was no familiar traffic noise – just the sound of the wind in the trees. That's when she realised that there were no street lights because there was no street. The car appeared to be parked in the middle of nowhere.

"Come on. Out you get," said Fran.

Sasha reluctantly did as she was told. It was only as her feet sank slightly into the damp, soft ground that she noticed the house. It loomed dark black against the paler black sky, like a spooky building in a horror film.

A shiver ran down Sasha's spine. She pulled her jacket tightly round her and folded her arms to anchor it in position. Then she stood with her shoulders hunched, waiting to see what would happen next.

Almost immediately a door opened at the side of the house, spilling out a pool of light that made the area beyond it seem darker than ever. Then two people stepped outside carrying torches and walked towards the car. Sasha couldn't see their faces properly, but she guessed from their outlines that the tall, broad shouldered one was a man and the shorter, slimmer one was a woman. These must be her temporary foster carers – the people who didn't really want her.

This is it, thought Sasha as she stepped back warily. *I wonder what's wrong with this lot*. There was always something. Reality had taught her that perfection didn't exist and that promises of staying forever didn't mean much either.

As the couple came closer, she braced herself in case they were the hugging type. To her relief, they weren't. They stopped a short distance away, and neither of them made any attempt to touch her – not even to shake hands.

"Welcome to Kingfishers," said the man. "Sorry it's so dark. The builders have messed up the security light."

Builders. Was that why they hadn't wanted to take her?

Her thoughts were interrupted by the woman's soft voice. "Come in, both of you. Joe can unload the car without our help."

Sasha wasn't so sure. Those were her things in the back seats. Would this stranger look after them properly? "I can do it myself," she insisted, grabbing hold of her rucksack.

"But you don't have to," said Fran in a firm, no-nonsense voice. "Joe can manage while we go inside and talk to Beth." She placed her hand on Sasha's back and pushed her gently forward.

Sasha resisted for a moment, hugging the rucksack close to her chest. Then she relented. Perhaps Fran was right for once. It might be easier meeting these new people one at a time.

Her senses were on high alert as she followed Beth up the path to the house. She heard the gravel crunch under her feet, felt a breeze blow against her cheek and noticed again that slight, almost-familiar smell.

It was stronger in the porch where a jumble of boots lay on the floor. Sasha was pleased to see they were all adult size. *No other kids*, she thought. Her recent experience with Cynthia had left her wary of foster carers with children of their own.

As she stepped into the kitchen, the nameless smell was drowned by the welcome scent of baking. It made Sasha's mouth water. So did the sight of a batch of cakes cooling on a wire tray. They looked promisingly like chocolate brownies. Maybe the food here would be better than at Georgina's.

Sasha glanced around, her anxious eyes taking in as many details as they could. The room was bright, cheerful and comfortably warm after the chilliness outside. Two walls were lined with kitchen units, a pine dresser stood against the third and a large, wooden table dominated the centre of the room. Jars and cookery books jockeyed for position on the shelves, a string of garlic dangled from a hook on the ceiling and a jumble of fresh vegetables filled the wicker rack in one corner.

But this kitchen wasn't just for cooking – the end of the worktop was piled with papers and magazines and a laptop computer stood open on the table. Sasha was pleased to see how untidy everything was. Maybe no one would care if her bedroom was as well.

"I'll make some tea," said Beth, as she switched on the kettle. "Are you hungry?"

Fran shook her head. "It's all right. We ate on the way."

"I could still manage some more," Sasha added quickly. Trust a social worker to say something stupid. Hadn't she seen those cakes?

"Great," said Beth. She took a plate from the side and started piling the brownies on it. "I'm glad I didn't waste my time making these."

"But you can't eat anything while you're hugging that rucksack," said a deep voice just behind Sasha.

Startled, she swung round and saw Joe had come in without her noticing. He gave her a brief smile. Then he strode past, swinging two bulging black sacks from each hand, and headed out of the kitchen. "Come on," he called over his shoulder. "You can put it in your room."

"That's a good idea," said Fran. "I'd like to see where you're sleeping."

You mean you want to inspect it, thought Sasha as she followed Joe into the hall. She was sure all social workers had forms to fill in when they got back to the office – ones with lots of boxes to tick. That would explain why they all asked the same pointless questions.

The landing at the top of the stairs was cluttered with boxes, ladders and pots of paint. "You'll have to excuse the chaos," said Beth. "We're still sorting out the damage done by the fire."

A fire. Fran hadn't said anything about that. Maybe that was what the strange smell was – smoke and charred wood. But surely if that was true, she'd notice it more inside the house than out.

Joe squeezed past the clutter, pushed open a door with his shoulder and switched on the light. Then he moved to one side to let Sasha go in first.

As soon as she stepped inside, she abandoned the idea of spending all her spare time in here. The room was far too small for that. There was hardly any space between the bed, the chest of drawers and the wardrobe. And there was no sign of a TV or a computer.

But it wasn't the collapse of her plan that made her throat tighten. It was the teddy bears that danced and somersaulted across the faded wallpaper. They were designed for a much younger child than her. Maybe it wasn't the fire and the builders that had made Beth and Joe not want to take her? Maybe it was her age. If they really wanted a toddler, she'd never be able to do anything right. She'd always be a disappointment.

"It's a lovely room," said Fran, with typical social worker brightness.

"No, it's not," said Joe, as he dumped the bags on the wooden floor. "It's too small and a bit scruffy, but it's the best we can do while our usual fostering room is out of action."

So the bears aren't for foster children, thought Sasha, not quite sure if that was good or bad.

Beth reached over the bed and pushed the window open. "This room's usually just a dumping ground for junk. A bit of fresh air will help clear the mustiness." She paused for a moment and looked outside. "It's a beautiful night now the sky's cleared. Come and see!"

Sasha thought it was a daft idea to look at a view in the dark. But she also thought it sensible not to say so. There was no point in annoying these people when she'd only just met them. So she knelt on the bed, put her rucksack down beside her and peered out of the window.

Beth was right. It was beautiful. The sky was full of stars – far more than Sasha had ever seen before. Beneath them, the world was shadowy and still. She breathed in deeply, filling her lungs with fresh, country air, and noticed again the smell she'd noticed when she first arrived. It was definitely stronger outside.

But this time, she finally recognised it. And that recognition gave her the first glimmer of hope she'd felt all day. As if in confirmation, a sound broke the silence – a sound that sent a shiver of excitement down Sasha's spine. It was the whinny of a horse.

Chapter 3

The whinny came again. "I expect that's Bella," said Beth. "She likes to let everyone know where she is."

"Is she yours?" asked Sasha, hardly daring to wait for the answer.

"Not exactly," Beth replied "We're just looking after her for a while."

Like me, thought Sasha. Did this couple make a habit of taking in other people's rejects?

Joe looked puzzled. "Didn't Fran tell you we train horses at Kingfishers? That's what Beth and I do for a living."

"She didn't give me a chance," Fran cut in quickly before Sasha had time to reply.

Sasha ignored her. She was too interested in Joe's words to care about the social worker's excuses. "How many horses have you got?"

Joe paused for a moment, counting silently on his fingers. "Twelve at the moment, including our own."

Sasha could hardly contain her excitement. Maybe this placement wouldn't be so bad after all. But that depended on the answer to one very important question. "Can I ride them?" she asked.

Joe hesitated and glanced at Beth. "We'll see," he said.

Sasha hated it when adults said that. It was just a way to put off saying "no". But this was so important that she tried again, more politely this time in case it made a difference. "Please let me ride. I know how to do it."

"That's interesting," said Beth. "None of our other foster children had had anything to do with horses before they came here."

"And they all rode in the end," added Joe. "So you might too."

That still wasn't a "yes", but it was an improvement. Sasha fought back the urge to keep pushing and stayed quiet. These people were still strangers – she didn't know how hard she could push them without making them angry.

Back in the kitchen, Sasha could think of little else except the prospect of riding again. She longed to bombard Joe and Beth with questions about the horses at Kingfishers. But she didn't want to irritate them so she kept quiet and concentrated on enjoying the brownies.

Fran dominated the conversation while they ate. Most of it was small talk, but some was official fostering stuff. Sasha concentrated on the horses inside her head and tried not to listen. She hated this bit of the handover – it made her feel like a puppy being given to new owners.

Eventually Fran got up to leave. "I'll find you another place as soon as I can," she told Sasha as they said goodbye beside the car. "But I'm sure you'll be fine here for a little while. And don't worry about school. There's no point in starting a new one for such a short time, so your teachers are going to send some work for you to do."

Sasha nodded, unable to trust her voice to remain calm. She didn't want the social worker to realise what a storm of emotions her words had caused. Delight at not having to go to school was mixed with fear of being left alone with strangers. And overwhelming both were anger and sadness at the unfairness of her situation. All her life she'd dreamed of being surrounded by horses. But now she was, she wasn't going to be allowed to stay.

That was the final straw for Sasha. Although she'd managed not to cry all day, her chest was tight now and she had a lump in her throat that made it hard to swallow. She knew she couldn't control her misery much longer, but she'd learned long ago that tears were not for sharing. They showed how lonely and vulnerable she was, and that was something she didn't want anyone else to know.

She forced herself to stay calm until she'd waved goodbye to Fran and watched her drive away down the unmade lane. Then she muttered something to Joe and

Beth about being tired and ran up to her room. She slammed the door behind her and threw herself onto the bed. Then her shoulders shook with sobs as she cried silently into her pillow.

By the time she stopped, she felt totally drained. Her nose was streaming, her eyes were red and her head ached slightly. The tightness in her chest and throat had cleared, but her fear and loneliness remained.

She forced herself to get off the bed and pull out the pyjamas she'd stuffed in the top of one of the black sacks. They were slightly damp where she'd wrapped them round her toothbrush but she put them on anyway. Then she opened the door and checked Beth and Joe weren't around before she crept to the bathroom. She didn't want them seeing her blotchy face and red eyes.

Everything felt so strange. The washbasin was a different shape to the one at Cynthia's. The soap smelt different, and the toothpaste tasted weird.

As soon as she was back in her room, she pulled the picture of her mum from her rucksack and stood it carefully on the bedside table. The sight of it was reassuring – something fixed in a changing world. And it helped the tiny room feel a little more like hers.

She stared at it for a moment. Then she jumped into bed and switched out the light. The room looked even stranger in the darkness. Spooky even. Sasha lay back, pulled the quilt up to her chin and tried to get comfortable. It wasn't easy. The mattress was harder than the one she was used to, and the pillow was thinner.

The bed creaked as she tossed and turned. The house creaked too – at least, she hoped it did. Otherwise there must be some other reason for the sounds she could hear. Not ghosts – she didn't believe in those. But mice maybe. Or another fire.

That last thought made her sit bolt upright, her stomach knotted with fear. A house that had caught fire once could easily do it again. She switched the light back on and listened hard, straining her ears for the crackle of flames. Then she noticed a white plastic box screwed to the ceiling. It was a smoke alarm and it looked brand new. Beth and Joe must have put it up after the fire.

Reassured by its silent presence, Sasha tried again to sleep. But her mind was too active. As she lay alone in the darkness, her thoughts tumbled over each other in their efforts to attract her attention. Was Fran right? If she hadn't exploded in rage this morning, would she still be at Cynthia's?

Yes, probably. But it wouldn't have been for long. That placement was a disaster, and the adoption was never going to happen. It hadn't been too bad at first. Georgina and Gerald had kept their promise about letting her learn to ride. But the lessons had stopped as soon as Cynthia didn't want to go any more.

She was the only one Georgina and Gerald really cared about. They wanted to adopt a polite, well-behaved sister for their beloved daughter, not a troubled almost-teenager with a mind of her own.

They'd have been better off getting a dog, Sasha thought angrily. *Poor animal!* Cynthia was nasty and spiteful and so were all her friends. Sasha had felt almost as alone there as she did now. And, once the riding lessons stopped, the only horse was the Shetland pony in the field across the road.

This place had to be better than that. Sasha smiled and stretched out in the bed, pushing her feet into the cold corners to claim ownership of the whole space. Kingfishers wouldn't feel strange once she got used to it. It was what she'd always wanted – a home with horses – and she needed to make the most of every minute of her brief stay. So tomorrow she was going to persuade Joe and Beth to let her ride, even if she had to stretch the truth a bit to do it.

Chapter 4

In the calmness that followed her decision, Sasha finally fell asleep. By the time she woke up, the rising sun had driven away the darkness and there was enough light to let her see the teddy bears dancing across the walls. She lay under the quilt, unsure of when to get up. She didn't know the morning routine here yet, and she didn't want to get into trouble for creeping around the house on her own.

Eventually she heard Joe and Beth go downstairs and took that as a signal that it was safe to do the same. She ran to the bathroom, tugged a comb through her hair and washed away the telltale traces of last night's tears.

As soon as she was back in her room, she rummaged in her black sacks, found the riding clothes Georgina had bought for her and put them on as quickly as she could. Then she grabbed her riding hat and slipped quietly down the stairs to the kitchen.

Joe wasn't there, but Beth was sitting at the kitchen table, writing on a laptop. She looked up when she heard Sasha come in and immediately noticed her riding clothes. "You are keen," she said with a smile. "But you need some breakfast before you do anything else."

"I'm not hungry," said Sasha. She didn't want to waste time eating. She wanted to get outside with the horses.

"But you're going to have something anyway," Beth said firmly. She waved a hand towards some packets on the worktop. "In this house, we usually help ourselves to breakfast. You can have cereal or toast – whichever you prefer."

Sasha chose cereal. It was quicker than waiting for the toaster to pop. She tipped a few cornflakes into a bowl, added a dash of milk and sat down at the opposite end of the table, as far as she could get from her new foster mother.

"You'll need a drink too," said Beth. She went to the fridge, poured a glass of orange juice and put it down in front of Sasha. "Did you sleep well?"

"Sort of," Sasha hedged. She felt uncomfortable with Beth so close.

Beth nodded sympathetically and went back to her seat. "It's not easy in a strange bed, is it? Maybe you'll manage better tonight."

Sasha wasn't sure if she needed to reply or not so she stayed quiet and stared through the window as she ate. She was disappointed that she couldn't see any horses from here. There were just some farm buildings and the unmade lane that led away from the house and vanished between some trees. That was the way out of Kingfishers – she'd seen Fran drive down it last night.

It was also the way in. Sasha was halfway through her cornflakes when she heard the sound of a vehicle grinding its way up the lane. A few seconds later, a lorry drove out of the trees. It had HORSES written above the cab in big black letters.

"Bother!" said Beth, as she jumped to her feet. "I wasn't expecting them this early." She turned to Sasha. "I'm sorry. I've got to help Joe. You'll have to finish your breakfast on your own." Then she ran out of the house, stopping briefly in the porch to put on her boots.

Sasha didn't want to stay in the strange kitchen on her own. She wanted to see what was in the horsebox. But she didn't want to get into trouble – not this soon after she'd arrived. She ran her new foster mother's words through her head, working out exactly what they meant. Beth had only told her to finish breakfast. She hadn't said anything about what to do next. Surely that was up to Sasha.

She shoved the rest of her cornflakes into her mouth and swallowed hard. Then she gulped down the orange juice, pushed her hat onto her head and ran outside, heading in the same direction that Beth had gone.

As she rounded the end of one of the buildings, she saw the horsebox parked in a concrete yard, close to a line of stables. Whatever was inside wanted to get out –

it was kicking and stamping so hard that it made the sides of the lorry shake.

Sasha stopped a few metres away, awed by the sheer fury of the sound. None of the three adults by the horsebox noticed her arrive. They all had their backs to her.

The driver was standing off to one side, watching Beth and Joe undo the bolts that held the back door shut. "Watch out!" he shouted above the din. "He's out of his mind. We had to drive him inside – he wouldn't let anyone near him."

"He'll feel better when he's out," said Joe, calmly. He reached up and took one side of the back while Beth took the other. Then they lowered it carefully to the ground and light streamed in through the open doorway.

The animal inside screamed with rage. Or was it fear. Sasha wasn't sure. She edged forward for a better look, her eyes fixed on the bay horse standing at the far end of the horsebox. His dark brown coat was soaked with sweat. His nostrils flared with each rapid breath, and his eyes were so wide open that the whites were showing.

He watched warily as Joe walked up the ramp towards him, carrying a headcollar. But as soon as Joe reached the top, the horse lunged towards him, snaking his head forward with his ears flat back and his mouth open.

Joe didn't flinch. Instead he spread his arms wide and yelled, "No!"

His reaction surprised Sasha. The horse seemed surprised too. He jumped backwards, snapping his teeth shut on empty air. Then he leaped forward again and rushed past Joe. His hooves thundered on the wooden ramp as he hurtled out of the lorry.

Sasha stood frozen in terror, like a rabbit caught in the headlights of a car. The horse was totally out of control and he was galloping straight towards her.

"Move!"

Joe's shout broke the spell, and she jumped sideways just in time. But she stumbled as she landed and lost her balance. As she fell, she felt the rush of air as the horse hurtled past without touching her – a racing blur of brown hair, black mane and tail and pounding hooves.

Sasha rolled as she landed, hoping she could jump straight back on her feet without looking foolish. But the impact knocked the breath out of her and she lay still for a moment. She couldn't hear the horse's hooves anymore – only her foster parents running footsteps.

Beth reached her a few seconds before Joe. She crouched down beside Sasha, her face white with concern – or was it anger. "Are you hurt?"

"I'm fine," said Sasha, forcing herself to sit up. But she knew she wasn't. Although she wasn't hurt physically, she was badly frightened and shaking from head to foot.

Beth put an arm round Sasha's shoulders to steady her. "It's okay. It's over."

Sasha stiffened at her touch. The sudden closeness didn't calm her at all – it made her heart race even faster. And Beth's soft words filled her with confusion. Why wasn't she shouting at her, telling her off for putting herself in danger? Georgina would have done. Everything had been Sasha's fault in Georgina's eyes.

Sasha clambered to her feet as fast as she could, twisting her body so Beth's arm fell away. That felt better – safer. "I'm sorry," she said, trying to take the edge off the scolding she was sure would come eventually. "I shouldn't have got in the way."

"I doubt if you will again," said Joe. "Not after a fright like that."

"And it's not your fault," added Beth. "You couldn't have known Meteor would act like that."

Meteor. So that's his name. Sasha glanced past Joe and spotted the horse standing on the far side of the yard, beside the post and rail fence that had blocked his escape. He was watching them warily, his head held high and his whole body poised for flight.

Sasha tensed too, ready to run if he came at her again. Instinctively she took a step backwards, trying to increase the distance between her and this terrifying horse.

"Don't worry," said Joe. "He won't do anything while we're ignoring him." He swung open the door to a nearby stable. “You can watch safely from in here while we get him in the paddock.”

Sasha was relieved to see the stable was empty. Much as she loved horses, she didn’t want to be close to one right now, however gentle. The incident with Meteor had shaken her confidence and, for the first time, she realised just how dangerous these animals could be.

Chapter 5

As soon as Sasha was safely inside the stable, Joe pushed the half door shut and turned his attention back to the runaway. Sasha gripped the top of the door with trembling hands as she watched him spread his arms wide again and walk towards the bay horse. Beth and the driver did the same, one walking towards him from the left and the other from the right.

Meteor snorted and swung his head from side to side, looking at each of the approaching humans in turn. He backed away from them for a few steps but was forced to stop when his rump hit the fence. There was no escape in that direction.

He spun round, searching for another way out. Beth, Joe and the driver were closer now. If he was going to get away, he needed to move fast. But where could he go?

Sasha noticed the gate at exactly the same moment that Meteor did. It was standing open a few metres from where he was standing, and she could see now that this was where Beth and Joe were trying to drive him.

Meteor leaped towards it at full speed and turned so sharply through the gate that Sasha thought he would slip. But he didn't. He galloped into the tiny paddock and kept going until he was at the other end, as far from human contact as he could reach.

Beth slammed the gate shut behind him. Then she beckoned to Sasha. "You can come over now. It's perfectly safe."

Sasha took deep breaths to calm herself while she walked across the yard and was pleased to find that she'd stopped shaking by the time she reached the others. They were standing side by side, watching Meteor.

She hesitated a moment, wondering where to go. There was a space between Beth and Joe that Sasha suspected they'd left for her. But it wasn't very big and she didn't like the idea of being squashed between these people she barely knew. So she slipped onto the end of the line instead, next to her new foster mother but not too close.

Beth smiled at her. "Are you feeling better now?"

Sasha nodded and turned her attention to the horse. Now he was the other side of a reassuringly strong fence, she felt safe enough to look at him properly for the first time. He looked scruffy and neglected. His brown coat was dull, his ribs stuck out and his black mane and tail were muddy and tangled. She couldn't understand why Beth and Joe wanted such an ugly, dangerous animal.

Neither could the driver. He shook his head as he watched Meteor and whistled backwards through his teeth. "I don't reckon you'll ever sort this one out. You should have let them put him down like they wanted to."

"Every horse deserves one last chance," said Joe.

"That's more than he'd get from me," the driver replied. He glanced at his watch and set off towards his horsebox. "I'd better be going. I've got two other jobs to fit in this morning."

Joe moved, as if he was going to follow him. Then he stopped and stared at Sasha, as if he had only just noticed what she was wearing. "You've got the right gear then. So do you really know how to ride?"

"Of course I do," Sasha replied without a moment's hesitation. This was her chance – the one she'd planned for last night when she couldn't sleep. She mustn't waste it. She crossed her fingers behind her back and added, "I've done loads of riding and I'm really good. My riding teacher told me so." She didn't mention that her riding teacher told everyone the same. She'd even said it to Cynthia just before she slid off Merrylegs and landed in a pile of manure.

Joe raised his eyebrows in mock surprise. "It sounds as if we've got an expert come to stay. I'd better see for myself. That's if you still want to ride after what happened just now."

"Of course I do!" said Sasha. Then she glanced at the horse in the far corner of the field and felt a shiver of fear run down her spine. "But not on him."

Beth laughed. "No one's going to ride Meteor for a long time. He's got a lot of learning to do before anyone gets on his back again."

"Pumpkin will suit you much better," said Joe. "I'll get him tacked up after the horsebox has gone." As he strode off towards the stables, he glanced back over his shoulder. "Meet me in the sand school in ten minutes."

Sasha hesitated, not sure what to do in the meantime. Then Beth walked off in a different direction and beckoned to her to follow. "Come and give me a hand while you're waiting. We need to give Meteor a feed to show him this is a good place to be."

Sasha wasn't sure she wanted to do anything for an animal that had almost trampled her. But she didn't want to stay beside his paddock on her own either. As she followed Beth across the yard, her stomach churned with a mixture of excitement and fear. She'd won. She was going to ride. But were all the horses at Kingfishers as scary as Meteor?

Beth led the way to a large, stone barn. Most of the inside was stacked with rectangular bales of hay and straw. But one end was partitioned off to form a feed room with large metal bins lining the walls.

"What's Pumpkin like?" Sasha asked, as she followed Beth into the room.

"He's fat and orange, just like his name suggests. And he's a real sweetie. I'm sure you'll like him." Beth picked up a black rubber bowl from a pile on the floor and thrust it into Sasha's hands. "He's our daughter's pony."

Sasha was so shocked that she nearly dropped the bowl. *A daughter! No one told me about a daughter.* "Won't she mind me riding him?" she asked, struggling to keep her voice calm. Cynthia had always minded Sasha using anything that was hers.

Beth laughed. "Of course not. We often use Pumpkin for riding lessons." She took a scoop that was hanging from a nail on the wall and turned her attention back to the feed. "I don't know what Meteor's been having up to now so we won't give him too much to start with. Just some chaff and a little bit of barley to fatten him up."

Sasha had no idea what either of these were, but she was sure it made sense to find out. So she pushed away her worries about this other girl for a moment and concentrated on what Beth was putting in the bowl. First, there was a whole scoop of what looked like chopped hay. Was that chaff? Then there was a handful of some sort of grain. *That must be the barley*, she worked out, making a mental note of which bin it came from. Learning horse care didn't seem too hard. But this daughter could be much more of a problem.

Beth tipped some water into the bowl from a watering can. "Now it just needs mixing," she said, as she handed Sasha a large plastic spoon.

For a moment, Sasha concentrated on stirring the contents of the bowl, watching the grains of barley disappear in the sweet smelling chaff. Then she asked the question that had been running around her head ever since Beth dropped the bombshell.

"How old is your daughter?" She tried to make her voice sound casual, as if she didn't really care. But she had learned the hard way that the answer was crucial – the closer they were in age, the more chance there was of trouble.

Beth looked surprised. "I'm sorry. I hadn't realised how little Fran's told you about us. Dawn's twenty now and away training to be a vet. She only comes home for occasional visits."

Sasha breathed a silent sigh of relief. At least their daughter wasn't going to be like Georgina's – mean and jealous and in her face all the time. That thought triggered memories of their last disastrous row, and she flinched as Cynthia's hurtful words echoed in her head again. *What if she was right? What if what she'd said was true?*

"Are you okay?" asked Beth, as they went back to the main part of the barn. "You seem upset."

"I'm fine," Sasha lied, forcing her mouth into a pretend smile. This woman was too observant. She'd have to be more careful in future if she wanted to keep her feelings to herself.

Her social worker would probably have pushed the point and asked more questions. But Beth appeared to take Sasha's answer at face value and went back to thinking about Meteor. "We'll take him some hay too. There's not much grass in the small paddock." As she spoke, she walked over to an open bale and picked up a generous portion.

Sasha watched her in dismay. She'd been planning to push the bowl into Beth's hands and make some excuse to escape – anything that would get her out of going near the bay horse again. But now Beth's arms were full of hay, Sasha had no choice. She had to carry the bowl back to the paddock.

Meteor spotted them long before they got there. He raised his head and watched them warily from the far end of the field. As they reached the fence, he put his ears flat back against his head, stamped one front foot and squealed.

The sound sent a wave of fear through Sasha's body. Her stomach knotted and she had to grip the bowl harder than ever to stop her hands shaking.

"Don't worry," said Beth. "He's not going to attack us. He's just warning us to stay away." As she spoke, the black horse spun round so his tail was facing them and kicked hard in their direction with both hind legs.

"See what I mean. That's horse language for stay out of my space."

Sasha didn't need any encouragement to do that. She didn't want to go any closer to Meteor than she was now. But she was puzzled by the horse's behaviour. When she'd visited the Shetland pony who lived opposite Cynthia's house, he'd always trotted over to the fence to see if she had any carrots for him. Why wasn't Meteor doing the same?

"Is he too grumpy to come over for his food?" she asked.

"I think 'too scared' is a better description," said Beth, as she tossed the hay over the fence. "Maybe he'll eat it when we've gone away."

Sasha pushed the feed bowl under the bottom rail so it was beside the hay. Then she looked again at the horse standing at the far end of the field with his tail still turned towards them. Surely Beth was wrong. Surely such a terrifying animal couldn't be scared of her.

Chapter 6

Sasha and Beth stood by the fence and watched Meteor for a while. But he didn't take a single step towards them or his food.

Eventually Beth turned away. "Come on," she said. "I've got to finish that article I was writing, and you've got to meet Pumpkin." She waved her hand towards the barn and added, "The sand school's behind there. You can't miss it."

Sasha wished Beth was going with her. She was still a stranger here, and her first attempt at exploring Kingfishers had almost ended in disaster. But the prospect of riding again was too good to miss so she set off in the direction Beth had shown her. She was glad she'd put on her riding hat when she left the kitchen. She wouldn't have wanted to waste time fetching it now.

She stopped at the end of the barn and peered round the corner to check she was in the right place. Beth was right – it was impossible to miss the large arena surrounded by post and rail fencing. And Joe had kept his promise. He was standing in the middle, holding the reins of the pony that stood beside him.

That must be Pumpkin. He certainly fitted the description Beth had given earlier. His chestnut coat was almost orange, and his body was very round. He was also very relaxed. Or maybe he was half-asleep. Either way, he looked much calmer than Meteor – more like the riding school ponies she was used to. Surely she'd be able to ride him without any trouble.

With renewed confidence, she stepped out of the shadow of the barn and went into the school. Joe saw her straight away and waved. "Come on over. We're all ready."

The sand was still damp after last night's rain. Walking on it reminded Sasha of a trip to the seaside long ago when she'd explored the beach after the tide went out. But that was with some other foster parents she could barely remember. And there were no ponies then. This was better.

Joe smiled when she reached him. "Say 'hello' to Pumpkin."

Still feeling nervous after her scare with Meteor, she held out her hand and let the pony sniff it. Sasha breathed in too, enjoying the warm smell of horse. *So far, so good.*

"You're sure you know what you're doing?" Joe asked, as he tightened Pumpkin's girth. "If you're not, I'd rather you told me now."

For a fleeting moment, Sasha wondered if she should tell him the truth. But she was so close to riding

Pumpkin now. She couldn't throw that chance away. So she crossed her fingers behind her back again and lied. "I'm a good rider. I told you that already."

There was a hint of suspicion in Joe's eyes. But he handed her the reins anyway and said, "Up you get. I'll hold the stirrup on the other side to make sure the saddle doesn't move."

Sasha's stomach tightened with nerves as she took hold of the reins. At the riding school, someone had always helped her get on from a mounting block. She'd never done it by herself from the ground before. But she didn't want to tell Joe that. Not now – not after she'd told him how good she was. He had to go on thinking she knew what she was doing or he might stop her riding before she'd even started.

She paused for a moment, trying to remember how she'd seen other, more experienced riders get on their horses. Then she put her left foot in the stirrup, grabbed hold of a chunk of mane and heaved herself onto Pumpkin's back.

She landed in the saddle with a bigger thump than she'd intended, but she didn't worry. At least she'd got there. That was the important thing. And it felt fantastic to be back on a horse again. She'd missed riding so much since Cynthia made the lessons stop.

As she pushed her feet down into the stirrups, her heart sank. They were much too long, and she wasn't sure if she could shorten them herself. That was something else that had always been done for her at the riding school.

Luckily, Joe volunteered without her asking. "I'll do those. The leathers are brand new and really stiff." He spent a while adjusting them to the right length. Then he stepped back and said, "Okay. Let's see how you get on. Start by walking him round the school."

Sasha sat up as straight as she could in the saddle and nudged the pony's sides with her heels. Pumpkin walked slowly forward until he reached the edge of the arena. Then he turned left without Sasha telling him to and started to amble along beside the fence.

Sasha tried to relax and let her body move in time with his. But she couldn't. She was too tense, too anxious and too aware that Joe was watching every move she made. Her mind raced, trying to remember everything she'd learned in those lessons. *Head up. Heels down. Shoulders back.* Why did her body have to have so many different bits? But she must get this right – she had to. This was her big chance and, if she blew it, she might not get another one.

She fiddled with the reins, trying to remember what length they should be. In the end, she decided longer would be better than shorter – she didn't want to hurt Pumpkin's mouth. The chestnut pony didn't seem to care. He wandered slowly on with his head hung low. All the riding school ponies had been quiet, but none of them had been quite this dozy.

"Change the rein at A," called Joe, when they'd ridden the whole way round the arena.

Sasha was pleased she knew what this meant. She waited until they reached the letter A marked on a post halfway along one of the short sides. Then she tugged on the inside rein and Pumpkin turned obediently up the middle of the school. That gave her confidence a much-needed boost – she felt more in control now.

The letter at the other end was a C. When she reached it, she tugged the other rein and turned Pumpkin so they were ambling in the opposite direction. Her sense of achievement grew.

Joe watched them go right round again before he said, "Now try a trot. Anytime you're ready."

Sasha wasn't sure if Pumpkin would ever be ready. He still seemed half asleep. She shortened her reins in the hope of attracting his attention. Then she kicked him hard in the sides like she used to with the riding school ponies.

Pumpkin woke up. He tossed his head in the air and bounded forward into a rapid trot. The sudden burst of speed took Sasha by surprise, and she grabbed hold of the front of the saddle like a complete beginner. Then she let go again quickly, hoping Joe hadn't noticed, and concentrated on trying to do rising trot. After a few uncomfortable bounces, she got the rhythm right and was relieved to find she could go up and down in time with Pumpkin's feet. That must be something you never forgot once you'd learned it – like riding a bike.

Joe watched them do two brisk circuits of the arena. Then he shook his head and said, "I don't think cantering would be a good idea. You seem a bit wobbly."

"I'm not," said Sasha. "I'm just a bit out of practice, that's all. I'll be fine cantering." She'd only done it twice before, but she remembered that she only had to sit still. There wasn't any up and down to worry about like there was with trotting.

"I'm still not convinced," said Joe.

"I can do it. Really I can. Watch me. I'll show you." Sasha shortened her reins again and gave Pumpkin another huge kick.

The pony shot off like a rocket – faster than Sasha had ever been before. The sudden acceleration threw her back in the saddle. Her legs shot forward, and she pulled hard on the reins – partly to slow him down and partly in a desperate effort to keep her balance.

Pumpkin pulled back even harder, jerking Sasha forward and almost pitching her over the pony's neck. She grabbed hold of his mane just in time to save herself. The reins slid through her fingers as the pony raced on, completely out of her control.

"Steady, Pumpkin," called Joe. "Trot!"

The chestnut pony flicked his ears in response to the order and did as he was told. But the trot was very fast and very bouncy. Sasha lost both her stirrups and felt herself sliding sideways in the saddle.

"And walk!"

To Sasha's relief, Pumpkin obediently followed Joe's instructions and the awful bouncing stopped. But it was too late for her to get her balance back. As Pumpkin finally came to a halt, she slithered slowly over his shoulder and landed on her backside in the sand.

Sasha wasn't hurt. But her mouth was dry and she was shaking from head to foot. The ride had gone completely wrong, and now she had to face Joe.

Chapter 7

Sasha scrambled to her feet, watching Joe's face as he strode across the sand towards them. He looked serious, but she didn't know him well enough to tell how angry he was.

As soon as he was close enough, he grabbed hold of Pumpkin's reins. Then he looked her straight in the eye and spoke in a low, firm voice. "I think it's time you told me the truth."

"I already have!" Sasha backed away from him, feeling her face redden under his gaze. But she stared back defiantly. "I didn't make it all up. I have had lessons." Then she paused, not sure if arguing was going to make any difference. She'd already had her chance and messed it up. "What happens now?" she asked.

"That depends," said Joe. "If you want to go on being arrogant and over confident and showing off, you won't be riding any of my horses again."

The 'if' at the beginning of his sentence gave Sasha a glimmer of hope. Was there a way out of this mess she'd got herself into? "And if I don't?" she asked quietly.

"If you admit you don't know everything, I might give you another chance. Now answer me honestly. How much riding have you done?"

"Not very much," Sasha confessed. "I have had lessons – that's true. But there were only twelve of them. And my teacher told everyone they were good, even when they were awful."

Joe's expression softened. "That's better. I hate being lied to. Now would you like me to teach you to ride properly?"

"Yes," said Sasha quietly. Then she added "please" just to be on the safe side.

"And you promise you'll always do what I tell you. No more showing off."

"I promise." And this time she didn't cross her fingers behind her back. She really meant what she was saying.

"Okay. That's settled. Now let's take Pumpkin back to his stable."

"Can't we start now?" Sasha demanded. That wasn't the deal. She was supposed to have a lesson.

"No," said Joe, with a firm edge to his voice that made Sasha regret arguing. "You'll have to wait until this afternoon. Pumpkin's done enough for now."

Sasha nodded, but said nothing. Silence seemed the safest option right now. This man controlled whether she could ride or not. It was important not to annoy him.

She walked the other side of Pumpkin as Joe led the chestnut pony out of the sand school and down a path behind the barn to a line of stables. These were different from the ones she'd seen before. They looked more modern and were built of timber instead of stone.

The door to the end stable was open. Joe pointed toward it and handed her the reins. "Take him inside. I'll fetch some brushes."

Sasha had never led a pony before, but she walked forward as confidently as she could and, to her delight, Pumpkin followed. As soon as they were in the stable, he dived for the bulging hay net hanging in one corner and started to eat as fast as he could.

"You can see why he's so fat," said Joe from the doorway. "He loves food."

He showed Sasha how to take off the pony's saddle and bridle. Then he gave her a brush and showed her how to clean off the mark left by the saddle. "It's usually safer to tie a horse up before you groom him. But you don't have to worry with Pumpkin. He's very well behaved, especially when he's eating."

"He wasn't well behaved when I rode him!"

"Yes, he was," said Joe.

"No, he wasn't. He went too fast."

"That's your opinion. It's not Pumpkin's. As far as he's concerned, he went at exactly the speed you told him to. He's only used to gentle leg aids. When you kicked him hard, he thought you wanted him to race off."

"But I didn't."

"I know that, but he doesn't," said Joe. "Horses are sensible animals. What they do always makes sense in their eyes and, if it's not what we want, that's usually our fault. It's the same with Meteor."

The mention of the black horse brought back the memories Sasha had pushed away. The sight of him hurtling towards her. The sound of his galloping hooves. And, most of all, the fear! "It's not my fault that he nearly ran me over," she declared, indignantly. "I didn't do anything. I was only standing there."

Joe smiled. "Don't worry. I'm not blaming you. I'm just explaining that Meteor wasn't born bad. Once upon a time, I'm sure he was like every other horse. But since then, he's had too many bad experiences and too many changes of home."

"So?" Sasha was becoming impatient. A troubled past wasn't an excuse for bad behaviour – that's what the social workers always told her.

"So Meteor's been so badly let down by humans that he doesn't trust any of us any more. He puts on a big act of being fierce to make people leave him alone. But deep inside, I'm sure he's scared stiff."

There it was again – that suggestion that Meteor was scared. First Beth had made it and now Joe. But Sasha still wasn't convinced. Meteor was the most terrifying horse she had ever met. If he was only pretending to be fierce, he was making a very good job of it.

When Pumpkin was settled in his stable, Joe sent Sasha back to the house on her own. "Ask Beth to put the kettle on. I'll be in as soon as I've done a couple of jobs."

Sasha was flattered to be trusted with a message and set off immediately. She remembered the way easily – down the path to the sand school and round the back of the barn. Kingfishers was already starting to feel more familiar.

She stopped at the far end of the barn. Meteor's field lay around the corner, and she wanted to look at the bay horse without him realising she was there. She put her hand on the rough stone wall to steady herself. Then she leaned forward and peeped around the corner.

Meteor had finally moved. He'd left the safety of the far corner and was now a couple of metres from the food she and Beth had left for him. As Sasha watched, he darted forward, grabbed a mouthful of feed from the bowl and ran off again. He stopped a few metres away and munched the food; his head still up and alert. Then he raced back to the bowl, took another mouthful and retreated again.

Sasha watched, fascinated. Perhaps Beth and Joe were right. Meteor certainly looked as if he was scared. And that wasn't so surprising. He'd been at Kingfishers for even less time than she had. Maybe he was just like her – trying to understand his new surroundings and trying to work out if anyone here was safe enough to trust.

He made five rapid trips to the bowl, running away a little less far each time. Then, on the sixth, he felt confident enough to stay beside it. But he still ate rapidly and lifted his head between mouthfuls to check he was still alone.

Sasha stood motionless in her hiding place. She was sure he'd run off again as soon as he saw her, and she wanted to give him a chance to finish his meal in peace. But when the bowl was empty, she knew she couldn't wait any longer. She still had Joe's message to deliver, and she didn't want to risk annoying him again.

Meteor was sniffing tentatively at the hay when she stepped out from behind the barn. She moved as slowly and gently as she could, but the horse reacted as if she was running at him brandishing a sword. His head flew up in alarm. Then he spun on the spot and galloped back to the far corner of the paddock.

As she reached the fence, he turned his tail on her, flattened his ears back against his neck and raised one back hoof in warning. But this time Sasha understood why he was doing it.

"Don't worry. I won't hurt you," she whispered, as she leaned over the gate. "I know how scared you are."

Chapter 8

It was halfway through the afternoon before Joe let Sasha lead Pumpkin into the sand school for her lesson. Having the chestnut pony walk beside her so willingly helped to calm her nerves. Maybe he'd understand what she wanted him to do this time. She didn't want him to run off again.

"We'll go slowly," Joe promised, as he checked the pony's girth. "You've been taught slightly differently from how we ride here. So this afternoon I'm going to show you our way."

As soon as she was safely in the saddle, he started teaching her how to sit correctly. Sasha struggled to do as she was told, but it was really difficult to remember everything at once. As soon as she got one part of her body in the right place, another shifted out of position.

"Don't worry. It will come," said Joe. "Now tell him to walk on. Just squeeze your legs against his sides – no kicking."

Sasha was surprised by how little she had to squeeze before Pumpkin walked forward, following the track around the arena. But there was no sign of the sleepy amble he'd done that morning. He moved more positively now she was telling him what to do correctly.

Although Pumpkin was doing better, Sasha wasn't. She sat stiffly in the saddle, desperately trying to stay in the right position, and she gripped the reins so hard that her fingernails dug into her palms.

Joe dotted some traffic cones around the arena and told her to weave Pumpkin in and out of them. "Don't tug on the reins to turn him. Just look in the direction you want to go and press your leg against the opposite side."

Sasha was sure that wouldn't work, but it did. And it felt good too. Pumpkin turned so neatly – much better than when she'd pulled him round with the reins that morning.

Her success helped her confidence grow, and she began to relax and sit deeper in the saddle. She loosened her grip on the reins a little. Her shoulders softened and so did her legs, but she kept her back straight and her head up.

"That's much better," said Joe. "And I'm not like your old teacher. I don't give praise when it's not deserved."

Sasha beamed. It felt good to finally be doing something right. As they moved on to trotting, she found that it only took a light squeeze to get Pumpkin moving at an easy pace: not too fast and not too slow. She rose up and down in time with his movement, but Joe wasn't satisfied.

"You're going up too high," he called. "That's why you're getting left behind and landing with a thud."

Sasha's smile vanished. She'd thought she was doing so well, but now it turned out that she wasn't.

"Don't go so high," Joe suggested. "You only need to get your backside clear of the saddle. And try rising slightly forward instead of straight up."

Sasha tried doing as he said and was surprised to find how much easier trotting was that way. Joe made her practise changing pace until finally she could get Pumpkin to change from walk to trot or trot to walk at exactly the mark in the school that he chose.

"That's a good place to stop," said Joe. "You've done really well. Now let Pumpkin walk on a long rein so he can stretch his neck and cool down."

Sasha didn't mind not cantering this time. She was tired and so was Pumpkin. The lesson had been much harder work than anything she'd ever had to do at the riding school.

As they walked slowly around the arena, Sasha breathed in the delightful scent of warm horse and gazed at the rolling green hills that surrounded Kingfishers. It felt so right – so absolutely and totally perfect – to be riding such a beautiful pony in such a beautiful place. For the first time she could remember, she was sure she was exactly where she ought to be.

A few minutes later, Beth came into the arena leading a palomino mare who was already saddled and bridled. "You look good together," she said, as Sasha jumped down from Pumpkin's back. "I'll help you turn him out while Joe rides Bella," She stroked the mare's neck and added, "She's coming on nicely, but she needs some more schooling before she goes back to her owners."

Her words brought Sasha back to reality. Bella wasn't staying at Kingfishers and neither was she. One day she'd have to say goodbye to all the horses and start again somewhere else.

They waited while Joe swung himself effortlessly onto the palomino's back. Then they walked Pumpkin back to his stable. Sasha was careful to keep the pony between them. She felt safer that way.

This time, Sasha succeeded in taking off Pumpkin's saddle by herself. She brushed his back thoroughly. Then she led him out to his field with Beth. The route took them past the sand school so they stopped for a moment to watch Joe working with Bella. He was practising changes of pace ('transitions' Beth called them), moving the horse from walk to trot to canter and back down to walk again.

It was a more advanced version of the exercise she had tried on Pumpkin. But Joe was controlling Bella with movements so light that Sasha could barely see them. "I'd love to ride that well," she said.

"You will if you try hard enough," said Beth. "I know you're only here for a little while, but you should be able to learn a lot in that time if you keep working at it."

"But what about after that? What if I can't ride at my next place?"

Beth smiled. "Riding's something you never forget. If you really like horses, you're sure to get back to them eventually – even if it's not until you're grown up."

"But that's years away!" Sasha blurted out, unable to keep the impatience out of her voice.

"So it's not worth worrying about," Beth said calmly. "Let's concentrate on enjoying today." As if to prove her point, she started pointing out the different wildflowers they were passing.

They led Pumpkin up a grassy path and through the gate into his field. It was much larger than Meteor's tiny paddock, and already contained several other horses. They all raised their heads to look at the new arrivals, but they quickly lost interest and went back to grazing.

Sasha unbuckled Pumpkin's headcollar and set him free. The pony wandered away a few steps and ate a mouthful of grass. Then he lay down on the ground and rolled.

"He's giving his back a good scratch after being ridden," Beth explained.

Sasha watched Pumpkin clamber to his feet again. Then she pointed to the other horses and asked, "Are they all owned by other people – like Bella?"

Beth shook her head. "No. All the horses in this field are ones we've bought cheaply because they had problems."

"Like Meteor?"

"That's right. But none of these were ever as bad as him. We'll sort them out and sell them on. All except Calypso." She pointed at a black horse drinking from the trough. "We've decided to keep him permanently."

Sasha pricked up her ears. So Joe and Beth did change their minds sometimes. "Why are you doing that?" she asked, trying not to show how much the answer mattered to her.

"Because he's so useful. He's got an amazing talent for jumping. He's just what Joe needs for his lessons and demonstrations."

Sasha said nothing. She was too busy wondering if the same thing that had worked for Calypso would also work for her. Maybe Joe and Beth would let her stay here with the horses if she could prove she was really useful. But how on earth could she manage to do that?

On their way back to the house, they walked past Meteor's field. Just as before, the bay horse fled to the far end as soon as he saw them coming. But Sasha could see he'd eaten nearly all his hay.

"That's a good sign," said Beth, pointing at the few wisps left on the ground. "We'd better get him some more."

Sasha immediately spotted her first chance to be useful. "Shall I get it?" she suggested.

"If you want to. But only bring one slice. That'll be enough for now."

Sasha ran off to the barn, wondering what that last instruction meant. Hay was nothing like bread? How could it be in slices? But everything made sense when she went up to the bale that Beth had used earlier. The block of tightly packed hay split naturally into sections – that must be what Beth was talking about.

She picked up a section in her arms and ran back to Meteor's field. The bay horse was still a safe distance away on the other side so she leaned through the fence and shook the slice so it came apart. The loosened strands of hay fell into a bouncy heap. But it didn't look much for such a large animal. "Shouldn't we give him more than that," Sasha asked. "He looks so thin."

"He can have some more later. If we feed him small amounts at regular intervals, he'll learn to associate us with good things instead of bad. That's how we'll start to build his trust."

"Can I do the feeding?" asked Sasha. "I'd really like to." That wasn't strictly true – she was still scared of the bay horse and didn't want to be near him. But she couldn't let fear stand in her way now. Winning

Meteor's trust would be a really useful achievement. Maybe they'd let her stay if she did that.

Beth looked doubtful. "That's a huge responsibility. He'll need hay and a feed morning and evening plus hay by itself at midday. And if you don't do it properly, you could do more harm than good."

"Please let me try," Sasha begged. "I won't let you down. I promise." And she knew this was a promise she had to keep. If she broke it, she might never get another chance to show Joe and Beth how useful she could be.

Chapter 9

Sasha had to repeat her promise again to Joe when he came back from riding Bella. He watched her face carefully as she spoke. Then he had a brief, whispered conversation with Beth.

Sasha hated it when adults talked about her as if she wasn't there, but she fought back her anger. It was easy to see how doubtful he looked and how hard Beth was trying to persuade him. She couldn't risk spoiling everything by losing her temper now.

Eventually Joe turned back to Sasha. "We think you mean it," he said. "And it would be useful if you took over feeding Meteor. So we're going to let you try."

Sasha's heart leapt in triumph. *Useful! He said "useful".* She just had to do this right. Then they'd be sure to tell her she could stay.

She was so sure she had made the right decision that she could hardly wait to get started. But, when the time came, Beth wouldn't let her fetch Meteor's evening feed on her own. She insisted on going with her.

"I can manage," said Sasha.

"I expect you can," Beth explained. "But I need to check that you know what to do."

Sasha stood in the middle of the feed room, trying to hold back a rising tide of panic. Having Beth watch her felt like a test, and she always messed up tests. But she had to pass this one – her future depended on it.

She took a deep breath to calm herself and tried to remember everything Beth had done that morning. She picked up a rubber bowl and swung open what she hoped were the correct bins. All right so far. Then she measured out the feed, just like Beth. One scoop of chaff and a handful of barley. Then a splash of water and a good mix.

"Well done," said Beth. "Now what about the hay?"

Sasha fetched a slice of hay from the same open bale she'd already used. But it was nearly finished – there was only one portion left for tomorrow.

"Which bale will you use next?" Beth asked.

Sasha pointed to one nearby, but Beth shook her head. "That's straw. See how thick and stiff the stalks are. Hay is much thinner and softer. Try again and see if you can get it right this time."

Stupid, stupid, stupid. Sasha could hear Cynthia's voice in her head, mocking her like she always did. But she pushed it away and tried again. Now she'd been shown the difference, she picked out a bale of hay without any problem.

Beth nodded her approval. "I'll carry the feed this time and you bring the hay. Tomorrow, you'll be on your own so you might have to make two trips."

Sasha could hardly contain her excitement. She'd done it. She'd passed Beth's test. So, from now on, she was in charge of feeding Meteor.

As the week went by, Sasha discovered that living at Kingfishers was even better than she'd hoped. With no school to go to, it felt like being on holiday. When she wasn't having riding lessons, she helped with the stable work or watched Joe and Beth train the horses. And every day she visited Meteor – taking him hay and a feed in the morning and evening, and hay by itself at lunchtime.

Every time she did it, the same thing happened. As soon as the bay horse saw her coming, he ran off to the far end of the field, turned his back on her and raised a warning hoof. However long she waited, he never came over to eat until after she'd gone.

Sasha became more and more frustrated by his behaviour. She was doing everything Beth had told her: feeding him at exactly the same times, always being quiet and never being threatening. But Meteor was still too scared to come close to her. Whatever had happened to him in the past must have been really bad.

By Friday morning, she was losing enthusiasm. Maybe the horsebox driver had been right. Maybe

Meteor was too damaged to help. She made up his feed in the barn and trudged off towards his field, with his slice of hay tucked under one arm and his bowl in her other hand.

Meteor was standing in the middle of the paddock, grazing. He lifted his head when he heard her footsteps. Sasha paused, waiting for him to spin on the spot and gallop off, like he always did. But today he stayed exactly where he was. He flicked his ears forward, flared his nostrils and stared straight at her.

Sasha stood completely still, hardly daring to breathe. Then very, very slowly she walked towards the fence. Meteor watched every step, but he still didn't move. Sasha crouched down and gently pushed the feed bowl under the bottom rail.

The horse still watched her, motionless. She wondered if she should give him the slice of hay just as it was, rather than risk scaring him by shaking it apart. But she didn't know if he'd be able to eat it like that, so she leaned through the fence and teased the strands loose with her fingers as quietly as she could. But, despite her care, it still made a rustling sound.

Meteor snorted and took a step back. But he didn't turn away, and he didn't gallop off. Sasha looked at him from the corner of her eye while she worked. This was the closest she'd been to the bay horse since the day he nearly trampled her. Was that really less than a week ago? She felt as if she'd been at Kingfishers much longer than that.

When she'd finished, she waited by the fence for a while, hoping Meteor would come over to eat while she was still there. But he wasn't ready for that yet. So eventually she left, as quietly as she'd arrived.

As soon as she was sure she was out of Meteor's sight, she broke into a run and set off to find Joe and Beth. It didn't take long. They were both in the yard in front of the timber stables. "You'll never guess what's happened," she yelled at the top of her voice.

Beth laughed. "If we'll never guess, you'll have to tell us?"

"And you don't have to shout," said Joe, putting his fingers in his ears. "I haven't gone deaf."

"Meteor didn't run away from me. He stayed in the middle of the field while I put his food by the fence."

Joe beamed at her. "That's brilliant! You must be doing a good job."

"Congratulations!" said Beth. She took a step towards Sasha, as if she was going to hug her or shake her hand or pat her on the head. .

Sasha didn't wait to find out which it was. She shook her head and ducked away, instinctively retreating to what she felt was a safe distance from both of them. She'd got to know them better during the last few days, but she still didn't feel safe enough to be touched.

A look of disappointment flitted across Beth's face for an instant. Then it disappeared as suddenly as it had arrived and was replaced with a big smile. "You're just the person we need right now. You can help us photograph Bambi."

Sasha knew that was the black and white horse that shared the field with Pumpkin and the other horses. "Do you want me to hold him?" she asked.

"No," said Joe. "Beth's going to do that. I want you to hold this." He handed her a carrot, cut in half lengthways. "Hide it behind your back and only show it to him when I say 'now'."

Sasha hid the carrot as she was told and waited while Beth fetched Bambi from his stable. He was a huge horse with a long, flowing mane and tail. His large hooves were almost hidden by the shaggy hairs around his feet – "feathers" Joe called them.

Sasha watched while Beth guided him into the right position for the photo. Then she took up position where Joe told her to go – straight in front of the horse but far enough away not to be in the picture.

Joe fiddled with his camera, trying to line up the perfect shot. Bambi was bored by the whole process. He looked at the floor. He looked at the sky. He looked everywhere but straight ahead.

Suddenly Joe called, "Now, Sasha."

Sasha brought the carrot out from behind her back and held it up high. Bambi spotted it straight away and his whole attitude changed. Suddenly he was paying attention. He raised his head, flicked his ears forward and looked straight at the food.

That's when Joe pressed the button on the camera. "Perfect," he said, as he checked the picture on the screen. "That will look great in the ad."

"What ad?" asked Sasha.

"The one for Bambi." Joe shoved the camera in the pocket of his jeans and explained, "He's improved so much since we bought him that he's ready to sell on now."

His words sent a shiver down Sasha's back. She'd always known that the horses moved on, but this was the first time she'd come face to face with the reality. She hated the idea of Bambi being sold, and that wasn't just because he would have to leave. It was also because it reminded her of how insecure her own future was.

She stepped closer to the huge horse and held out the carrot on the flat of her hand. His lips felt velvety on her palm as he gently took it from her. He was so calm and trusting. He had no idea that his world was about to change. "Won't he mind going?" she asked.

"Maybe for a day or two," said Beth. "But he'll soon settle in. We always make sure our horses go to good homes."

What about your foster children? Sasha wondered silently. *Do you do the same for them?* She was definitely going to mind if she had to go. And it wouldn't just be for a day or two. It would be forever. She was sure of that.

Chapter 10

When they had finished photographing Bambi, Joe went back to the house to load the pictures onto his computer. Beth went with him, claiming she needed to work on another article and do some cooking. But Sasha stayed behind.

Discovering that Bambi was leaving was a painful reminder that her own time at Kingfishers was running out as well. Although she'd made a bit of progress with Meteor, it was taking much longer to gain his trust than she'd expected. Maybe she should find some other ways to be useful too.

She wandered into the tack room and looked around at the saddles and bridles hanging on racks on the walls. Perhaps she could clean some of them. That would definitely be useful. And it wasn't that hard. Beth had already shown her how to do it so Sasha was sure she could manage it by herself.

She picked out the dirtiest bridle. It was the one that had come with Meteor, and it looked as neglected as he did. The leather was stiff and hard with disuse so it was difficult to undo the buckles. But Sasha persevered until she had taken the bridle apart. Then she fetched a bucket of water, wiped all the pieces with a damp sponge and laid them on the tack room table. They dried quickly in the warm air and looked much cleaner. But they were still hard and stiff.

Neatsfoot oil. That's what Beth had said was good for softening leather. So Sasha fetched the can from the shelf, took off the lid and brushed a liberal coating of oil onto each part of the bridle. Then she added a second coat in the hopes of making a thorough job.

The leather was definitely softer now. But it was also dripping with oil. She'd have to give it time to soak in before she could use any saddle soap. She left the can of oil on the table and looked around the room for something to do while she was waiting. A pile of old lead ropes lay jumbled up in one corner. Sorting those out would be a useful task – one that was sure to please Beth and Joe.

She wriggled between the saddle racks and the table, reached into the corner and picked up the pile of ropes. Moving them sent a cloud of dust into the air. Sasha had expected that. What she hadn't expected was the huge spider than ran out from the middle of the pile and scuttled across her hand.

Sasha hated spiders. She dropped the ropes and jumped away, shaking her hand violently. She was concentrating so hard on getting rid of the horrible creature that she didn't look where she was going. She crashed into the table, jolting everything on it.

"No!" She lunged forwards, trying to catch the open can of oil. But she was too late. It tumbled onto its side, sending its contents cascading across the wooden tabletop and over the edge onto the floor.

Sasha grabbed the tack cleaning sponge and tried to mop up the ever-increasing puddle. But it was a hopeless task. The sponge was far too small to absorb so much oil.

She looked around, desperately searching for something better. Then she spotted the ideal thing – an old towel Joe used for drying saddles when they'd been out in the rain. It was draped over an empty saddle rack just a couple of metres away.

She rushed towards it without thinking. Her foot landed in the slippery puddle of oil and slid out from underneath her. She tried to save herself by grabbing at a headcollar hanging on the wall. But all she did was knock it off its hook. As she landed on the floor, the headcollar fell on top of her and draped itself over her head.

At that moment, a shadow fell across Sasha. She looked up and saw Joe standing in the doorway, blocking the sunlight.

His eyes narrowed as he surveyed the mess. "What on earth's going on?"

Sasha cringed away from him, trying to get her excuses in quickly before he lost his temper. "I didn't do it on purpose. I was trying to clean Meteor's bridle, but there was a spider and the oil fell over and now everything's a mess."

"I can see that," said Joe. Then he burst out laughing. "Don't look so worried. It's not the end of the world." He held his hand out to her. "Come on. Up you get."

Sasha carefully avoided taking his hand and clambered to her feet by herself. As she did so, she breathed a sigh of relief. Thank goodness Joe thought her mistakes were funny. Georgina and Gerald never had.

Joe tossed the towel to Sasha. "You wipe the floor, and I'll put the bridle back together. We need to clear this up quickly – you're needed back at the house."

"Why?"

"Fran's come to see you."

Sasha concentrated on mopping up the spilt oil, hoping he didn't notice her twinge of alarm. Was this just a routine visit or had her social worker found her somewhere else to live? Somewhere without horses.

With both of them working, they only took a few minutes to straighten the tack room and set off for the house. They found Fran sitting at the kitchen table, drinking coffee with Beth.

"Hello," she said as Sasha went in. "How are you settling in?"

"Okay," said Sasha with a shrug. If Fran wanted more information than that, she'd have to work harder to get it.

"That's good, because I still haven't found anywhere else for you to go."

Sasha said nothing, hoping that Joe or Beth would cut in and tell Fran she could stop looking. That Sasha could stay at Kingfishers forever. But they didn't.

Fran opened her bag and pulled out a camera. "I'm going to put an ad in the fostering and adoption magazines. So I need to take some photos of you."

Sasha scowled. "Just like Bambi."

Fran looked totally confused. "What's a Disney film got to do with anything?"

But Beth understood. "It's not the same, Sasha. No one's trying to sell you."

"It feels like they are. I hate being advertised. Last time it happened, I ended up with Georgina and Gerald." Her voice was getting louder and she could feel the anger rising in her. If she wasn't careful, she'd explode with rage, and she didn't want to do that. Not here. Not in the place she wanted to stay.

Joe intervened, speaking in the calm voice he used for worried horses. "Why don't you go upstairs and clean up? You don't look very photogenic at the moment."

Glad of the excuse to leave, she ran out of the kitchen and up to her room. A quick glance in the mirror showed her that Joe was right. Her T-shirt and jeans were grubby with oil and dirt from the tack room floor. Her face was almost as bad and her hands were filthy.

She cleaned herself up in the bathroom while she took some deep breaths to calm down. Then she put on clean jeans and her least favourite top – the one that didn't suit her. The worse she looked, the greater the chance that no one would reply to the ad. And, if there was nowhere else for her to go, Joe and Beth would have to let her stay here with the horses. Wouldn't they?

When Sasha finally went back to the kitchen, Fran jumped to her feet with her camera in her hand. She pointed towards a waiting chair. "Sit over there. The plain cream wall will make a good background."

Sasha sat stiffly, her back rigid with tension. She was hating every minute of this and didn't feel remotely like cooperating.

Fran held up the camera. "Now, smile!" she said in her sweetest voice.

Sasha didn't. Instead she pushed out her bottom lip in a determined pout. What was the point of pretending? If prospective foster parents wanted to see her photo, they might as well see her looking bad tempered and stroppy.

"Sasha, please," Fran pleaded. "Do try. Just one little smile."

She replaced the pout with a scowl. Then Joe jumped to his feet, waving a chocolate brownie in exactly the same way that she had waved the carrot at Bambi.

It was a silly joke and he looked so ridiculous that Sasha couldn't stay bad tempered any longer. She burst out laughing, and Fran clicked the camera.

"Isn't that lovely?" she said, as she showed everyone the picture on the screen.

Sasha was disappointed to see that it was. The girl in the photo looked happy and friendly – just the sort of child someone might want to take into their home. Maybe the ad would get some replies after all. And then she'd have to leave.

Chapter 11

Fran put away her camera and asked Sasha to take her on a tour of Kingfishers. Sasha wasn't fooled – she knew the real reason for their walk. Visiting social workers were supposed to talk to her by herself, away from her foster parents. Some of them didn't bother. But Fran always stuck by the rules, and today she was using the tour as an excuse to do it.

It soon became obvious that Fran was out of her depth in the countryside. She wrinkled her nose as they passed the muck heap and trod carefully to avoid getting mud or manure on her shoes. She also kept well away from the horses, even fat little Pumpkin.

"He won't hurt you," said Sasha, as the chestnut pony put his head over the gate to greet them. She ran her hand down his face and let him nuzzle her fingers. "Look. He's really gentle."

"He is with you," said Fran, from a safe distance. She sounded as if she expected him to turn into a fire-breathing dragon if she went any closer. "I'm glad you're settling in all right with Joe and Beth."

"It's great having all the horses." Sasha hesitated for moment, wondering if this was the right moment to say more. Then she decided she had to risk it, even if the timing was wrong. "I'm sick of moving. Can't I stay here forever?"

Fran sighed. "I'm afraid forever's not an option. Joe and Beth only take short-term foster children, and right now they're not even sure they want to go on doing that."

"But they took me."

"Only as a special favour because there was nowhere else for you to go. And I've promised to move you on as soon as I possibly can." She gave an unconvincing smile. "Don't worry. I'm sure the advert will find you a lovely new family."

"With horses," Sasha declared so firmly that Pumpkin flicked his ears in surprise. "There must be horses. You've got to put that in the ad."

"I can't do that. It would make you even harder to place. But I will try to mention that you like them."

"I don't just like horses. I love them."

Fran shook her head in puzzlement. "I've never understood the attraction horses have for some people. A couple of my friends have tried to get me interested in theirs, but it didn't work. They're just big, smelly animals that are dangerous at both ends. I can't see what all the fuss is about."

Sasha stared at her in disbelief. Was this woman a complete idiot? How could anyone not like horses?

She cut the rest of the tour short. There seemed no point in showing Fran the other animals or telling her about this morning's success with Meteor. She wouldn't be interested.

Sasha was relieved when they got back to the house. She was even more relieved when Fran turned down Beth's offer to stay to lunch. She would have happily said "goodbye" there and then in the kitchen, but Joe and Beth insisted she went outside with them to see the social worker safely on her way.

Fran was about to get into her car when she stopped and turned to Sasha. "I nearly forgot. I've brought something for you." She walked round to the back of the car and opened the boot.

Sasha peered round her, eager to see what was inside. Was it a present? Or something she'd left behind at Cynthia's? Then she spotted the large bag of books, and her heart sank.

"Your old school is being wonderfully helpful," said Fran, as she lifted out the heavy bag and thrust it into Sasha's unwilling arms. "They've sent all your books and some work for you to do. When you've finished, you can post it back and they'll mark it and send you some more."

Sasha groaned. "Do I have to?"

"Of course you do," said Fran. "You can't avoid being educated. It's the law. You either do lessons at home or you go to the school in the next town. And I don't think it's worth starting there when you'll be moving again very soon. Unless you want to, that is."

"I don't," Sasha replied immediately. She didn't need time to think about that decision. She'd been to too many schools already and been shouted at by too many teachers. She just wished she could opt out of studying at home as well.

As soon as Fran had driven away, Sasha carried the bag indoors, hoping to hide the books in her bedroom and forget all about them. But Joe stopped her on the way through the kitchen.

"Put them on the table while we have another coffee. I'd like to see what you're doing at school."

"So would I," said Beth, as she lit the gas under a pan of home-made soup. "If you start straight away, you can get some of your work done before lunch."

Sasha didn't like that idea at all. She dumped the bag of books on the table with a loud thud. Then she sat down on the chair furthest from Joe and Beth, and folded her arms defiantly. The mere mention of school had brought back a host of unpleasant memories that danced around her head. She could hear Cynthia's voice again, shouting *Stupid, stupid, stupid*, and she could feel her anger rising again, just like it did when that happened for real.

Joe put a fresh cup of coffee in front of her. Then he picked up the top book and flicked through its pages.

"They make history much more interesting than they did when I was your age."

"History's boring," grumbled Sasha, without looking at him.

He picked up two more books. "How about science or maths?"

"Boring, boring, boring."

Beth reached into the bag, pulled out a bundle of worksheets, and held them out to Sasha. "Have a look and see what they're asking you to do."

"I don't want to!" Sasha scowled and pulled her folded arms more firmly into her chest.

"It doesn't matter what you want," said Joe. "Fran's already told you that." He took the worksheets and plonked them down on the table in front of her. "Now choose one and get started."

Sasha said nothing. She stared angrily at the worksheets, her fists clenched and her shoulders tense as the memories whirled in her mind. Why did social workers always spoil everything? She'd been so happy here until Fran arrived with the horrible schoolwork. Now Beth and Joe would find out the truth, and they wouldn't like her any more, just like everyone else.

Joe pointed at the top sheet. "Why don't you start with that one? It's maths, so I expect you'll need this." He held out the maths textbook he was holding and waited. When Sasha didn't take it, he spoke again in his firmest voice. "You can't just sit there. You've got to finish this sheet before today's riding lesson or there won't be one."

That threat was the last straw. The memory of Cynthia's voice in her head rose to a crescendo, blocking out everything else. *You're so stupid even your mother didn't want you,* it screamed. And Sasha exploded.

Burning with rage, she grabbed the maths book from Joe's hand and flung it across the kitchen as hard as she could. It crashed into the dresser, smashing one of the storage jars and sending two others tumbling to the floor where they broke as well.

The sound of breaking glass was followed by a stunned silence. Sasha stared in horror at the destruction she'd caused. Then she jumped up from her chair and rushed out of the room.

She raced up the stairs two at a time, and ran into her bedroom. Desperate to be alone, she slammed the door shut and leaned back against it, taking deep breaths to try to quiet her racing heart. She'd blown it again. She knew she had. This was every bit as bad as what she'd done at Cynthia's, and she could remember only too well what had happened after that.

There was no point in hanging around, waiting for the ultimatum she knew would come. So she stomped over to the wardrobe, pulled out the black sacks she'd stuffed into one corner and started to pack.

Chapter 12

One by one, Sasha pulled out all the drawers and tipped their contents onto the floor. Then she knelt beside the untidy heap and started tossing her clothes into the black sacks without bothering to fold them. She didn't care if they were creased up when she got to the next place. She didn't want to think about the next place at all. Leaving here was going to hurt. She'd already given her heart to the horses.

The first sack was only half full when there was a loud knock on the door, followed by Beth's voice. "Are you all right in there?" she called.

"Go away!" Sasha didn't want to see her – she wasn't sure she could hide how she was feeling. "I'm busy."

"Doing what?" Beth threw open the door and rushed in. Her eyes widened as she spotted the heap of clothes in the middle of the floor. "Give me the matches!" she yelled, thrusting her hand under Sasha's nose.

Sasha was so surprised that she dropped the socks she was holding. "What are you talking about?"

"The matches!" Beth yelled even louder. "Give them to me."

"I can't," said Sasha, cringing away from the angry onslaught. " I haven't got any."

That's when Beth noticed the black sacks. She sighed with relief and lowered her outstretched hand. "You're packing!" she said in a more normal voice. "You're not trying to start a fire."

"Of course I'm not. What made you think I was?"

Beth sank down onto the bed. "It's what happened last time. With Zack – the foster child we had before you. The one who set fire to the house." She paused, staring at Sasha's puzzled expression. "Let me guess. Fran didn't tell you about *that* either."

"No," said Sasha, as she picked up the socks again. Now she knew about Zack, she understood why Beth was worried about matches, why there was a brand-new smoke alarm in her bedroom and why the usual fostering room was out of action. But she didn't understand what made Zack screw everything up. "I don't light fires," she said, as she picked up the socks again. "It's a daft thing to do."

"But you do throw things. Fran warned us about that."

Sasha tossed the socks into the sack and sat back on her heels. "I don't plan to. It just happens when I get really, really angry."

"Maybe you should do the running up to your room first in future – before you explode with anger. That way you'll only smash your own stuff, not mine."

Sasha felt a glimmer of hope. Was there a hint in those words that she might not have to go? Maybe this was the right moment to apologise. "I'm sorry about your jars. I can buy some new ones if you like. With my pocket money."

"That sounds fair. And I'm glad you've said sorry. Now are you sure you want to go on packing?"

Sasha shook her head. "I don't want to go. I'd much rather stay." She didn't say "forever" – that might be pushing things too far right now.

Beth smiled. "We're not going to throw you out over a bit of broken glass. You can stay a bit longer – until Fran's advert works its magic and finds you somewhere else."

"Thanks," Sasha said quietly. Her relief at not having to leave was tinged with disappointment. This was only a temporary reprieve. She'd still have to go eventually. She picked up some clothes from the floor and started shoving them back in the drawers.

"I'll give you a hand," said Beth. She slid off the bed and knelt on the floor beside Sasha.

Sasha stiffened instinctively. Something deep inside her said "No". That this was too close. That she'd be safer at a distance. She edged away slightly and muttered, "I can manage by myself."

"I'm sure you can. But sometimes it's nicer not to." She picked up a T-shirt, folded it neatly and tucked it into a drawer. "And while we tidy up, we can talk about your schoolwork. Throwing that book didn't make it go away."

Sasha felt the anger stir again. "I don't want to do it!"

"I got that message loud and clear. What I don't understand is why?"

Sasha said nothing as she glanced sideways at Beth's face. There was something about this woman she liked. Maybe it was her calmness. Maybe it was the gentle way she spoke. But was that enough. Could she really trust her with the truth?

It was Beth who broke the silence. But she didn't do like Fran and just repeat the question Sasha hadn't answered. Instead she asked something completely different. "How many different schools have you been to?"

"Lots. I've not bothered to count. I've changed school every time I've moved home and I've moved lots of times."

"I bet that makes it hard to learn," said Beth. "Different teachers teach different ways, and they're not always in the same place in a topic. I wouldn't be surprised if you're a bit behind with your schoolwork?"

"More than a bit," Sasha whispered. She was surprised Beth had guessed so much of her secret. She held her breath, worrying that she might work out the rest. And what would happen then.

Beth sat back on her heels and looked at Sasha thoughtfully. "Have you been told you're stupid?" she asked.

Sasha considered lying. But what was the point? Beth wasn't going to believe her – she was far too good at working out what Sasha was thinking. "Stupid, stupid, stupid. That's what Cynthia said all the time." She didn't mention the bit about her mum. That was too private, too personal.

Beth wrinkled her face in disgust. "What a nasty spiteful girl! No wonder you weren't happy living with her."

"But she was right, wasn't she? Other people have said it too."

"And they were all wrong," said Beth. "I can see you're not stupid. You're learning about the horses really fast."

"That's different. I'm rubbish at school. I can't do anything."

"That's not because of you. It's because you haven't been taught properly. I reckon you'd be able to do as well as everyone else if you caught up all the stuff you've missed."

Sasha sighed. "There's not much chance of that. I wouldn't know where to start."

"But I would," said Beth. "I used to be a teacher a long time ago. Before..." Her words died away as she stared into the distance.

"Before what?" Sasha asked.

Beth jumped slightly, as if Sasha's words had woken her from a dream. "Before we moved to Kingfishers," she said quickly, her voice back to normal. "Before we started training horses."

Sasha was sure there was something else. Something Beth was keeping back. She'd seen that look before when kids at the children's home remembered people they'd lost. Had Beth lost someone too?

Her thoughts were interrupted by Joe's voice. "Is everything all right up there?" he shouted from downstairs. "Only this soup's boiling like mad, and I'm not sure what to do with it."

Beth jumped to her feet, laughing. "Leave it for me," she called back. "Everything's fine. I'll be down in a minute." Then she turned to Sasha. "I meant what I said. I'll help you with your schoolwork if you want me to."

"Okay," said Sasha. It was worth a try. She couldn't possibly make a worse mess of those worksheets with Beth's help than she would without it.

Beth looked genuinely pleased. "We'll start as soon as you've finished up here," she said, as she headed for the door. "Right now I need to sort out that soup before Joe ruins it. He's the world's worst cook."

Sasha watched her leave. Then she turned her attention to the heap on the floor and went back to tossing the clothes into the drawers. But she couldn't stop thinking about what Beth had said. No one else had ever suggested that Sasha's failure at school wasn't her fault. And no one else had ever offered to help. Was there really a chance that Beth could make a difference?

Chapter 13

Beth didn't believe in wasting time. She sat down at the table as soon as Sasha arrived in the kitchen. "Come on. We can get started while the soup simmers."

Sasha settled herself in her usual place, facing the dreaded bag of books. Beth moved her chair uncomfortably close and picked up the maths worksheet Joe had chosen earlier. It was about percentages.

"I can't do those," said Sasha. "They're too hard."

"They're certainly not easy," Beth agreed. "Do you know what percentages are?"

Sasha shook her head. "No one's ever told me. The other kids already knew about them when I started at my last school, but I didn't."

"See!" said Beth, beaming in triumph. "That's just what I said must have happened. We've found our first gap in what you know. Let's see if we can fill it." She fetched some paper and pencils. Then she started to explain how percentages are about dividing things into a hundred pieces.

Sasha listened carefully. Working one-to-one like this was much better than being in a class at school. And Beth's explanations were so clear that for the first time ever Sasha managed to work out a few simple percentage sums correctly. She had to use a calculator because her arithmetic was awful, but she still found it very satisfying to see Beth put large ticks beside her answers. She was much more used to crosses.

"Well done," said Beth. "Now let's look at that worksheet again." She thrust the paper into Sasha's unwilling hand. "Read out the first question and see how you get on with it."

Sasha's stomach knotted with panic as she stared at the jumble of letters and numbers on the page. Her mouth went dry, just like it did when she had to read aloud at school, and she could feel her anger rising. But she mustn't explode again now – not when she'd been given another chance.

She swallowed hard, picked up the sheet and started reading, slowly and hesitantly. Her face reddened with embarrassment as she stumbled over the words. *Stupid, stupid, stupid.* Cynthia always made fun of her at times like this.

But Beth didn't. Instead she leaned back in her chair and looked thoughtful. "Do you always find reading that hard?"

Sasha nodded, her shoulders slumped in defeat. "I must be stupid. That's why I can't read as well as everybody else."

"That's not true." Beth's voice was calm and reassuring. "You've just not had a chance to learn."

"Really?"

"I'm positive. Reading is just another gap we need to fill – a really important one. Does it cause a lot of problems at school?"

Sasha nodded again. "I can't read the worksheets fast enough so I get left behind."

Beth flicked through the rest of the homework. "I see what you mean. Struggling with these isn't going to do you much good at all." She dumped the worksheets and books back in the bag and pushed it away. "How would you feel if we just give all this back to Fran next time she comes?"

"Brilliant! So I haven't got to do any schoolwork after all?"

Beth laughed. "Oh, no! I'm not letting you off that lightly. I'm just thinking it might be better if I set the work for you. If we concentrate on English and maths, we can really sort out those gaps you've got."

"Even the reading?" Sasha asked doubtfully.

"Even that. So what do you think? Is it going to be the school's lessons or mine?"

"Yours," said Sasha without a moment's hesitation. Beth was a good teacher. She'd already helped Sasha with her maths. Maybe she really could help with everything else too.

Beth smiled as she went over to serve the soup. “That’s great. Let’s see how much better you can get while you’re here.”

There it was again – another reminder that Sasha’s stay at Kingfishers was only temporary. That one day she would have to move again. Nothing she had done so far had made them change their minds about that. But now it wasn’t just the horses she would be losing. She’d be giving up Beth’s help too.

The soup was carrot and coriander – thick and delicious. Sasha dropped chunks of crusty bread into her bowl, dunking them with her spoon until they’d absorbed as much as they could and then popping the soggy pieces in her mouth one by one. As she ate, she listened to Joe and Beth reviewing the progress of the different horses and planning the next stages of their training.

Eventually the conversation turned to the bay horse. “Meteor’s filling out a bit,” said Joe, “but he needs more time before he’ll trust us.”

“He already trusts me,” said Sasha, spotting a chance to point out how useful she was. “He didn’t run away today when I took him his food.”

“I know,” said Joe. “And that’s really good. But it’s just the first small step. We can’t do any serious work with him until we can catch him.”

That's it, thought Sasha. *That's what I've got to do. If I manage to catch Meteor, they'll be so impressed that they'll be sure to let me stay.*

Filled with enthusiasm, Sasha set off to see Meteor as soon as she'd finished eating. There was no point in wasting time. The sooner she caught him the better.

She went to the tack room first and picked up a headcollar that looked the right size. Then she fetched his usual slice of hay from the barn and walked towards his field with the headcollar slung over her shoulder.

Meteor was grazing in the middle of the field. He raised his head when he heard Sasha's footsteps and flicked his ears towards her as he watched her approach. But he didn't run away, and he didn't look scared. Instead, he stood still, looking calm and relaxed as he whisked away a fly with his tail.

Sasha pushed the hay under the fence as usual. Then she stood on the bottom rail, leaned over as far as she could and called, "Here, Meteor. Come on, boy. Come and say hello." She was sure she could slip on the headcollar if she could persuade him to put his head over the fence.

The change of routine took Meteor by surprise. He arched his neck and took a step backwards, his eyes fixed on Sasha and his whole body tense.

"Come on," Sasha called again, patting her thigh to encourage him in the way that often worked with dogs.

But it didn't tempt Meteor. He tossed his head and took another step away from her.

Sasha was disappointed. But she couldn't give up now – not when success was so tantalisingly close. She picked up a handful of hay and held it out towards him. "Come and eat," she called and waved the hay to show him how lovely it was.

The sudden movement was more than Meteor could cope with. He snorted with alarm, spun round and raced off to the farthest corner of the field. Then he turned to face her again, watching her cautiously and obviously wondering what she would do next.

Sasha started at him in dismay. Catching him wasn't going to be as easy as she'd hoped. Now she knew he wouldn't come to her, she had no choice. She had to go into the field with him.

A shiver ran down her back as she remembered the last time there had been no fence between her and the bay horse. That was the day Meteor arrived – the day he'd galloped out of the horsebox and nearly trampled her. The thought of putting herself in that situation again was terrifying. But the thought of leaving Kingfishers was awful too.

Shaking with fear, she climbed over the fence and slid down to the ground on Meteor's side. She was so scared that she could hardly breathe. But she went on anyway, walking slowly towards the horse. "Steady, boy," she said as calmly as she could.

The horse stood rooted to the spot as he watched her come closer and closer. She was near enough now to see his nostrils flare with each rapid breath and notice the damp sweat marks on his neck. Meteor was even more scared than she was.

Instinctively Sasha did what she would do to a scared human to show she wouldn't hurt them. She threw her arms wide apart with her hands open to show she was unarmed. But that didn't make Meteor calmer. Instead, it seemed to frighten him even more. He squealed in terror and galloped away.

"Stupid horse," she yelled, as she watched him hurtle around the edge of the field in panic. She'd failed completely, and she had no idea what to do next.

Chapter 14

"Just leave him!" Joe's voice made Sasha jump. She'd been so intent on catching Meteor that she hadn't noticed she was being watched. Now she was sure she was in trouble. Joe beckoned to her from the other side of the gate. "Come out now. He'll calm down quicker if you're not there."

She checked where Meteor was to make sure she wasn't crossing his path. Then she ran over to Joe and slipped through the gate to join him. "I'm sorry," she said, before he had a chance to tell her off. "I was only trying to help."

Joe raised his eyebrows and smiled. "You seem to be making a habit of doing that today. First the tack room disaster and now this."

"Aren't you cross?" she asked.

"Surprised – yes. Worried – a bit. But cross – no. Why should I be? I hadn't told you not to go into Meteor's field, and we had talked at lunchtime about needing to catch him. I just hadn't expected you to try."

"He wouldn't let me near him."

"I noticed. Now let's go and put that headcollar away." Joe strode off towards the tack room and Sasha fell into step a safe distance to one side of him.

"Why did he run away?" she asked, when they arrived.

"He's not ready yet. He needs to know you a lot better before he'll let you touch him, and a lot better still before he'll let you take away his freedom by putting this on him." As he spoke, he took the headcollar from Sasha's hands and hung it on a hook on the wall.

"But how can he get to know me if he won't come near me?"

"Just keep doing what you're doing. Taking him his food three times a day lets him get used to you being around without putting any pressure on him. I'm sure he'll let us touch him eventually. But you've got to be patient. Healing damaged horses like Meteor can't be rushed. It takes lots of time."

Sasha choked back the scream of frustration that rose to her throat. *But time is what I haven't got.* If she was going to change Joe and Beth's minds by catching Meteor, she had to do it before Fran's horrible advert found her another home.

As she walked back to the house, she knew that somehow she had to speed the process up. Her future depended on it. And the obvious way to do that was to spend more time with Meteor, even if that did risk putting more pressure on him.

But she had to be careful. Joe had been quite clear that three times a day was enough. If he thought she was rushing the horse, he might stop her doing anything with him at all and that would ruin her plan completely.

When Sasha took Meteor his evening feed, she was pleased to see that her failed attempt at catching him hadn't damaged his fragile confidence. He stood still in the middle of the field while she walked over to the fence. Then he watched as she pushed his feed bowl underneath and shook his hay into a tidy pile beside it.

Usually she walked away at that point to make him feel safe enough to come and eat. But today she lingered, gazing carefully around the field in search of the perfect place to spend extra time near Meteor – somewhere the bay horse could see her easily but Joe and Beth couldn't.

A lone tree stood straight and tall on the far side, its branches spreading wide to give shade from the sun. But the area around the tree was too easily seen from all directions, and, although its leaves offered a good hiding place, the trunk was too smooth and bare to climb.

Three sides of the field were no better – just the bare post-and-rail fence with no hiding places at all. But the fourth side was lined with bushes of various shapes and sizes that provided shelter from the wind and hid the fence from the house.

Sasha set off to explore with high hopes, but those were soon dashed. Most of the bushes turned out to be hawthorns crammed tightly together and covered with unpleasant prickles that tore at Sasha's face and arms when she tried to squeeze between them.

She was almost on the point of giving up when she found two bushes of a different variety that were thorn-free and more welcoming. She pushed between them and discovered a small clearing just beside the fence. Meteor's field lay straight ahead so she could see the horse and he could see her. But behind her and on either side a wall of green branches waved gently in the breeze, completely blocking her from sight. This was the perfect spot to spend more time with Meteor. No one in the house or yard would ever see her here.

Life at Kingfishers felt less like a holiday after Fran's visit. The lessons with Beth saw to that. But she was a good teacher who pitched the work at exactly the right level. As the days whirled past, Sasha found that, for the first time she could remember, she was actually learning. Her riding was improving too and so was her knowledge of horse care.

Life wasn't standing still for Bambi either. His advert came out on Thursday, a couple came to see him on Friday and he was gone by Monday. He left for his new home as happily as Beth had promised, but Sasha found the whole process made her feel sick with fright. If she couldn't persuade Joe and Beth to change their minds, would she have to leave Kingfishers just as quickly?

To her relief, there was no news about her ad. She was starting to hope that Fran had forgotten all about it when an envelope dropped through the door one morning during breakfast. It was addressed to Sasha and contained a large glossy copy of her photo, a folded cutting from a magazine and a postcard from Fran.

The postcard had a lovely picture of a chestnut pony on one side and a handwritten note on the other.

Dear Sasha,
I hope you like this picture and you are being good. Here is the advert we talked about. Please give this photo to Beth because she asked for it.

Best wishes
Fran

Fran had written the words in large, clear letters, but Sasha still took some time to read them. When she finally finished, she muttered, "This is for you," and pushed the photo over to Beth. Then, very reluctantly, she picked up the magazine cutting. The last ad had landed her with Georgina and Gerald. What damage would this one do?

She was tempted to screw up the cutting and throw it away unread. But that wouldn't help – other copies of the ad were out there for people to read. She already had so little control of her life that she should at least check up on what her social worker was doing.

She forced herself to unfold the paper and was shocked to see her own face grinning back at her under the heading "Sasha needs a home". That was more than she could cope with. She threw the cutting down again in disgust.

Beth picked it up. "Shall I read it out for you?"

Sasha nodded and listened in increasing dismay to the words her social worker had written. It sounded hideously like the ads for horses in Beth's magazines. But instead of saying "good to shoe, hacks out alone or in company", it rambled on about "challenging behaviour" – whatever that was. Worse still, it didn't say anything about her love for horses, not even at the end. How dare Fran leave that out.

"That's horrid," Sasha yelled. "I wish she hadn't sent it."

"I'm not surprised you're upset," said Beth. "I don't think I'd like to be advertised like that."

"But it will be worth it if it finds you a lovely new family," said Joe. "I'm sure Fran knows what she's doing."

"I'm not," snapped Sasha. "She'll place me with any family that answers the ad, just like they did last time. I don't think it would have mattered if Georgina and Gerald had been little green men from Mars."

Joe burst out laughing. He put his hands on his head and waggled his fingers like antennae, while he put on a silly, alien voice and chanted, "Take me to your social worker."

Sasha couldn't help laughing too. He looked so funny. And it was impossible to laugh and be angry at the same time.

"That's better," said Beth. "And remember – it wasn't Fran who sent you to them. I'm sure she'll be more careful than that."

Joe thoughtfully swirled the last of his coffee in his mug. Then he gulped it down, pushed his chair away from the table and stood up. "Do you want to come up to the sand school, Sasha? There's something I've been meaning to show you and doing it now will take your mind off that advert."

Sasha hesitated. She was dying to know what this mysterious thing was, but she didn't want to get into trouble. "I'm supposed to be doing maths after breakfast. Beth said so."

Beth smiled and waved at her to go. "Maths can wait for a while. Let me know when you're back."

Delighted to be free, Sasha followed Joe out of the house and across the yard. But they didn't go straight to the sand school. Instead, they went to the stables where Joe put a headcollar on a beautiful, black Arab and led him out into the sunshine.

"Why do we need Kermit?" Sasha asked. She'd watched Joe working with the young horse before, but she'd never had anything to do with him herself.

"He's going to help you learn about body language," Joe explained, as he led the horse towards the sand school. "When I watched you trying to catch Meteor the other day, it was pretty obvious you don't know much about it."

"Was I that bad?"

"Yep! You treated him like a human and he's not. Horses use body language differently from the way we do. If you want to work with them, you've got to start thinking like a horse."

Chapter 15

Joe led Kermit into the middle of the sand school and waited until Sasha had shut the gate and walked over to join them. Then he reached up, unbuckled the Arab's headcollar and slipped it off. Kermit wandered away for a few steps and shook his head as if he was enjoying his newfound freedom. Then he turned and walked towards Sasha.

Sasha glanced sideways at Joe, wondering what to do.

"Just stand still," he said. "He's not met you before so he's checking you out."

Kermit came right up to Sasha and stopped. Then he rubbed his head hard on her chest, nearly knocking her off her feet. Without thinking, she stepped backwards to keep her balance.

"Does that feel comfortable?" Joe asked.

"No. I'm not a scratching post. I want him to stop."

"So tell him so. He's testing you out to see if he can make you move your feet. If he can, he'll think he's in charge. If he can't, he's more likely to think that you are."

At that moment, Kermit started to rub himself on Sasha again. “No!” she said, but he took no notice. He rubbed so hard that she lost her balance again and took another step backwards.

“It’s no good. He’s not listening.”

“Yes, he is. But you’re not speaking horse. Next time, just slap your thighs really hard and take a step forward.”

Sasha wasn’t at all sure that would make any difference but it was worth a try. As Kermit started rubbing his head on her for the third time, Sasha stepped towards him and slapped both hands hard against her legs. It made a louder noise than she’d expected, and Kermit jumped back in surprise.

“Good,” said Joe. “Now *you’re* moving *his* feet.”

The black horse came back for one more try. Sasha did exactly the same as before and he jumped back again. He wandered away a few steps and looked at her. Then he came forward again.

Sasha was poised to slap her legs again, but it wasn’t necessary. Kermit didn’t rub against her at all this time. Instead, he stepped sideways and stood motionless beside her. He looked calm and relaxed with his head hung low.

“Why’s he doing that?” she asked.

“He’s accepted you,” Joe explained. “Horses are herd animals and right now you’re part of his herd. Try walking away and see if you can get him to go with you.”

Sasha turned so she was facing the same way as Kermit. Then she said, "Walk on," and stepped forward. To her delight, Kermit stepped forward too. Soon they were walking round the edge of the arena together with Sasha slightly in front.

"Now see if you can stop him," said Joe. "Use your voice and your body to tell him what to do."

"Whoa!" said Sasha as she stopped walking herself. Kermit ambled on for a few paces on his own. Then he gradually came to a halt and looked back to see what she was doing.

"You forgot the body language. Try again, and this time make it really obvious what you want. Bend your knees and sink your body down a bit like a horse would move his back legs when he was stopping at speed."

Sasha caught Kermit up and walked forward with him again. Then she tried another stop, doing just like Joe had said. She was stunned by how perfectly it worked. Kermit stopped dead with his eyes fixed on her, waiting for the next instruction. And it wasn't just a fluke. She tried the same process twice more, and he behaved perfectly each time.

"That's amazing! Have you trained him specially?"

"No," said Joe, with a shake of his head. "He's just behaving like a horse. If he was in a wild herd, he'd stop when his leader told him to. His life might depend on it. And right now, you're his leader."

Sasha stroked Kermit's neck to tell him what a good boy he was. This was huge fun – almost better than riding. "What are we going to do next?" she asked.

"We're going to give him a break. We'll walk over into that corner without encouraging him to follow us."

Kermit seemed to understand that he didn't have to walk with them this time. He watched them walk away. Then he wandered off and sniffed a pile of manure left from the day before.

By the time Sasha reached the corner, Kermit had stopped taking any notice of her. The manure had lost its appeal, and a bird in a tree had caught his attention.

"Okay," said Joe. "We've now got much the same set-up as you had when you tried to catch Meteor the other day. Except that you know Kermit isn't scared of you. So I want you to walk straight towards him and, when you're halfway there, I want you to throw your arms wide apart with your palms towards him, just like you did with Meteor."

Sasha turned and walked straight towards Kermit's head, slowly but confidently. He'd already accepted her so she was sure she'd be able to catch him easily. He watched her closely as she approached, but he didn't look worried.

She counted her steps in her head, trying to judge the distance perfectly. When she was sure she was halfway, she threw her arms apart in the gesture of innocence she'd used to show Meteor she wouldn't hurt him. To her amazement it had exactly the same effect on this horse as it had on him. Kermit snorted with alarm, spun round and galloped to the other end of the sand school.

Sasha's shoulders slumped as she watched him race away. "What have I done wrong?" she called to Joe.

He came up beside her, his long legs covering the distance between them in a few strides. "You're using the wrong body language. Opening your arms wide like that is a good way to show other humans that you mean no harm. But horses interpret it completely differently. It makes you look like a big, scary predator who's coming to grab them."

"So Meteor and Kermit both ran away because they were frightened of me."

"Exactly," said Joe. "If you want to get close to a nervous horse, you need to do the exact opposite. Turn away from them slightly to make yourself look as small and non-threatening as possible. And don't aim straight for their head. That's their vulnerable spot – the place the lion aims for. It's less threatening to walk in a curved line and go towards their shoulder."

"Does that really work?" Sasha asked doubtfully. She couldn't see how such a small change could make enough difference.

"Try it now with Kermit. Take the headcollar this time and see if you can put it on."

The black horse was still at the far end of the school, but he looked calmer now. He shook his head, sending his long mane tumbling in all directions. Then he grabbed a mouthful of grass that was growing through the fence and started to munch it.

Sasha took the headcollar in her hand and swivelled round so her left shoulder was facing Kermit. Then she started walking vaguely in his direction, choosing a curved path across the sand that was designed to end her up close to the horse. She kept her eyes down, but glanced sideways now and again to see what Kermit was doing.

Before she was halfway, he had finished eating and was watching her carefully. She stopped for a moment to give him time to relax and was pleased to see him take another mouthful. Maybe this was going to work after all.

Closer and closer she walked until she was near enough to touch him. But she didn't. She paused again, giving him time to get used to her being there. Then she gently reached out and scratched his shoulder, just as she'd seen Joe do earlier. Kermit tensed at her touch and then relaxed.

"That's right," said Joe softly. "Now work your way slowly up his neck and show him the headcollar. But whatever you do, don't try to grab him. You'll just spook him again, and you'll never manage to hold him once he's decided to go."

Sasha stroked his neck, starting close to his shoulder and working her way along until she was almost at his head. It would be so simple now to just throw the rope around his neck or grab hold of a piece of mane to stop him escaping. But Joe was right – she wasn't strong enough to hold him by force. She could only catch Kermit with his agreement.

She took the headcollar in both hands and held it up to the horse, fully expecting him to run away. But he didn't. He stood absolutely still while she slipped the straps over his nose and fastened the buckle behind his ears.

Kermit looked so gentle now – more like the horse she'd had the fun with earlier than the one that had fled from her first attempt to catch him. "You're a good boy," she soothed, as she stroked his face.

"And you're a good girl," said Joe, who'd walked over just in time to hear what she was saying. "You got the body language right that time."

Sasha felt a glow of pride — she'd really achieved something this morning. Next time she tried to catch Meteor, she'd know the right way to do it. But she'd have to judge the time exactly right. She didn't want to try again too soon and have another failure.

Chapter 16

"I'm back," called Sasha. She ran into the living room, still glowing with pride about her success with Kermit. "Joe's been teaching me how to catch horses."

"That's good," said Beth, who was standing beside the bookshelves that lined the far wall. She pulled out a book with a horse on the cover and showed it to Sasha. "I loved *Jill's Gymkhana* when I was your age so I'm sure you'll like it better than any of the books your previous teacher suggested."

Sasha was sure she would too. English at her old school had been really boring, just like everything else she did there. But Beth had a way of making lessons interesting, and she wove horses into them as much as she could.

As they walked out of the room, Beth waved her hand towards the framed photos that crowded together on top of the piano. "Look what I did while you were out."

Sasha was thrilled to see the latest addition to the collection. It was the photo of her – the one Fran had sent – but now it was mounted in a white and gold frame that matched the others. Seeing it there made her feel that she belonged, that she was really part of the family.

"Do you know who the other people are?" Beth asked.

"I'm not sure," said Sasha. She'd looked at the photos before, but, until today, she'd never found a good time to ask about them. "Is that you and Joe?" she asked, as she pointed at a picture of a young couple getting married.

Beth nodded. Then she looked more closely at the photo and laughed. "Don't we look young? And the fashions look ridiculous now."

Sasha wasn't sure if she should agree or not. So she moved along the line of photos and pointed at a teenage girl with curly hair the same colour as Beth's. "Is that Dawn?"

"Good guess! That was taken at college last year. You might meet her next time she comes home for a weekend, if you haven't moved on by then."

There it was again. Another reminder that this stay was only temporary. Why did that always happen just as Sasha was feeling more secure? But at least Beth had said "if". Maybe everything wasn't settled. And her picture was on the piano. That must mean something.

The next photo in line was of a baby dressed in a pink dress with white frills. "Is that Dawn when she was younger?" Sasha asked.

Beth sighed. "No. That's Jennifer, our other daughter. She died when she was two months old."

Sasha felt awkward, sure she should say something but unable to decide what words to use. "I'm sorry," she said eventually, only too aware that this was a pretty weak response to something as important as death.

"So am I," said Beth. She paused and did that wistful look again – the one Sasha had first seen on the day Fran brought the schoolwork. "But I've got used to it now. And it all happened such a long time ago."

Sasha was silent for a moment while she searched for a way to change the subject to something more comfortable. Then she waved her hand towards three photos standing on the other side of the wedding picture. "Who are they?" she asked, desperately hoping they were still alive.

"They're our other foster children – the ones we had before you."

They're all boys. Was the fact Sasha was a girl a problem in Joe and Beth's eyes? If it was, she was going to have to work even harder to persuade them to keep her.

Beth pointed at a red-haired lad with freckles and a toothy grin. "Carl was the first. He was eight when he came here." Her finger moved on to the next picture: another boy with brown skin, dark curly hair and a grin as big as Carl's. "And that's Eddie. He was nine. They're both happily settled with their new families now."

She hesitated at the last picture. It showed an older boy with a mop of dark hair that flopped forward over his face. His mouth was smiling, but his eyes weren't. They looked dark and troubled. "That's Zack. He was the same age as you."

And he set fire to the house, thought Sasha. Maybe being twelve was a bigger problem than being a girl. "Where is he now?" she asked.

"In a special unit for disturbed children," Beth said quietly. "We tried really hard, but we couldn't help him. He was already too damaged when he came – too emotionally frozen."

Sasha had no idea what she meant by that last comment. What she did know was that Zack's photo was still on the piano, even though they'd thrown him out. So she was wrong. The fact that hers was there didn't increase her chances of staying at all. She'd have to do that herself.

As soon as they were back in the kitchen, Beth announced that it was time for lessons. She was a brilliant teacher, but Sasha found it harder than usual to concentrate. Her mind kept going back to that awful advert.

Suppose someone was looking at it right now – someone with a daughter as nasty as Cynthia? Suppose they wanted her. How long had she got before she had to move again and leave the horses behind forever?

It was a huge relief when Beth finally said she could go. Sasha immediately slipped away to her secret spot beside Meteor's field. She needed time to think and that was her favourite place to do it.

The bay horse looked up when he heard her wriggling through the bushes to the fence. She sat on the top rail and called him as usual. But, as usual, he didn't come over.

Ever since she'd found this spot, she had spent every spare minute here, trying to get Meteor used to her. But she hadn't succeeded. After that first initial breakthrough when he stopped running away, he remained as wary of human contact as he always had been and he still refused to eat while Sasha was close to his food.

She watched him carefully as he lost interest in her and went back to grazing. He seemed content to live the rest of his life just as he was, accepting what he needed from people but refusing to give anything back in return. Was that what Beth called being emotionally frozen? Was Meteor too damaged to help, just like Zack?

Chapter 17

Despite her doubts, Sasha didn't give up with Meteor. There was too much at stake to do that. She was still sure that catching the bay horse was the best way to prove to Joe and Beth how useful she was. And she was still sure that being useful was the key to being allowed to stay at Kingfishers.

But nothing she did seemed to make any difference to Meteor. Her frustration grew worse and worse as two more weeks raced past without any change in his behaviour. To her relief, there was also no news of the advert. Although Fran phoned a couple of times to check Sasha was all right, she never mentioned it at all.

Sasha clung to the hope that no one would reply and concentrated on enjoying her life at Kingfishers. Fortunately, her lack of success with Meteor wasn't echoed in anything else she did. Her maths was gradually improving, her reading was more confident and, best of all, her riding was going from strength to strength. She wasn't restricted to the sand school any more, and she loved exploring the countryside on Pumpkin's back when she rode out with Joe or Beth.

The next Monday started well. The weather was gorgeous, lessons went smoothly and Joe took her on the best ride she had ever had. When she got back, she burst into the kitchen, bubbling with excitement. "Guess what! We galloped all the way up Buckberry Ridge. It was brilliant. I've never been that fast before."

Beth looked up from her laptop and smiled. "Did Pumpkin enjoy it too?"

"He loved it." Sasha opened the fridge and poured herself a glass of milk. Then she sat down on a chair at the opposite end of the table. Although she tolerated sitting close to Beth for lessons, she still preferred to stay a safe distance away the rest of the time.

"Fran phoned while you were out. She's coming over this afternoon about four."

"Does she have to?" groaned Sasha. She didn't fancy another tick-the-boxes talk with her social worker.

"She says she's got some good news for you."

Sasha stiffened. The advert. It must be the advert. "Did she say what it was?" she asked, trying not to let her fear show in her voice.

Beth shook her head. "She wouldn't tell me. She wants you to be the first to know."

Sasha swallowed hard and tried to stay calm. Maybe she was worrying about nothing. There must be other things Fran would consider good news. Maybe it was something about school. No, it couldn't be. Beth knew more about that than the social worker did.

The more she thought about it, the more convinced she became that her first guess was right. Someone had answered the advert – some stranger who had offered to give her the new home she didn't want. Fran would be sure to think that was really good – the best news ever. But for Sasha, it would be the worst news of all.

Time was running out. If her plan to persuade Joe and Beth to keep her was going to succeed, she couldn't delay any longer. She had to try to catch Meteor today, before it was too late.

But, if they realised what she was planning to do, they might try to stop her. So she decided to wait until after lunch. Joe and Beth would expect her to go to see Meteor then so they wouldn't be suspicious.

She ate her lunch in silence, ignoring Joe and Beth's attempts to draw her into the conversation. She didn't want to think about anything except the task ahead. She kept running the memory of catching Kermit over and over in her mind, picturing every step so she could use exactly the same technique with the bay horse.

It was a relief when lunch was over, and she had the perfect excuse to escape. "I've got to feed Meteor," she said, as she jumped up from the table. "I don't want to keep him waiting."

As soon as she was outside, she ran and fetched a headcollar from the tack room and a slice of hay from the barn. Then she set off towards Meteor's field. He was standing on the far side in the shade of the big tree, idly whisking his tail to keep the flies away. He looked up when he saw her coming and watched her shake the hay into a pile. But he didn't move towards her.

Sasha took a deep breath and put her hands on the fence, ready to climb over. Then she changed her mind and stopped. This wasn't the right place to begin. Meteor was used to seeing her in her secret spot. He'd seen her climb onto that bit of the fence lots of times, so he wouldn't be surprised if she did that today.

She walked around the outside of the field to the line of bushes and pushed her way through the branches to the hidden clearing. Then she climbed up and sat on the top rail as she always did. Meteor watched her, but he didn't seem worried. So she summoned all her courage and slid down on the other side.

She'd hoped she would be less frightened than she was before. But she wasn't. As she landed on the grass, her heart was pounding and the palms of her hands were damp with sweat.

Meteor seemed so much scarier now there was no fence between them to protect her. Remembering what had happened the day he arrived, she slipped the headcollar off her shoulder and held it tight in her left hand. Maybe she could use that to frighten him away if he galloped straight at her again.

She stood for a moment, working out the route she was going to take across the field – not straight, like she did the first time, but slightly curved so she didn't look as if she was going to attack. She turned her body sideways, facing her left shoulder towards Meteor, so she looked as small as possible. Then she swallowed hard to steady her nerves and set off, walking slowly but steadily along her chosen path. Meteor watched her warily, but he stayed where he was.

The nearer she got to him, the more powerful the horse looked and the more frightened she became. By the time she was almost close enough to touch him, she was so scared that she could hardly breathe. Her mouth was dry and her stomach was knotted with nerves. But she tried hard to look calm. She straightened her back, forced herself to smile and pushed her free hand deep into her pocket to hide the fact it was shaking.

Meteor wasn't fooled. He arched his neck and backed away, his nostrils flaring with each rapid breath.

"Steady, boy," Sasha called. "It's only me." She kept her voice soft and gentle, but it shook slightly, making her nervousness even more obvious.

Meteor started to panic. He took three more rapid steps backwards, his eyes so wide with fear that the whites of his eyes showed.

Sasha panicked too. She was frustratingly close, but she could see he was about to run. She had only seconds left to act or she would lose him. So she did the only thing she could think of. She ran forward and tried to grab him.

Her sudden movement was the last straw for Meteor. He squealed with fright and spun on the spot. Then he galloped away, his tail held high as his feet pounded across the paddock.

Sasha flung the headcollar to the ground in a flash of temper. But she was angry with herself, not Meteor. Joe had warned her never to try to grab a horse, but she'd done it anyway. Now Meteor was terrified. There was no chance of her catching him today or maybe any other day either.

She checked Meteor was a safe distance away. Then she picked up the headcollar, ran back to the fence and climbed over. She felt calmer when she reached the safety of the other side. The fear had gone and so had the anger. But the despair remained. She'd failed completely, and Fran would be here soon with the news Sasha was dreading.

Chapter 18

Sasha could see no point in spending more time with Meteor now. Getting to know him hadn't made any difference. He was still as unapproachable as ever. So she trudged back to the house and spent the rest of the afternoon half-heartedly tidying her room.

Fran's visit started the same as usual. She arrived late claiming the traffic was horrendous, just like she always did. And Beth and Joe asked her in for coffee and cake, just like they always did.

As the four of them sat around the table, eating and drinking, Sasha listened impatiently while the adults chatted. What was the point of all this small talk? It was just delaying the moment of truth – the moment her social worker revealed why she'd come.

Eventually Fran licked the last traces of chocolate brownie from her lips, leaned back in her chair and looked straight at Sasha. "I've got some really good news for you."

"Will I think it's good too?" Sasha asked, hoping desperately that she'd guessed wrong. That this news was something different – something that didn't mean moving.

"I hope so." Fran paused dramatically before she announced, "I've found you a lovely new home. One where you can stay forever."

Sasha stared at her in horror, her last hope dashed. Now her worst fears were realised, she felt too stunned to react.

Fran reached into her briefcase and pulled out a photo album. "Your new foster parents are called Sue and Tom Weaver. They're really keen to take a girl your age and I'm sure you'll like them. They're a lovely couple."

Lovely, lovely. Doesn't this woman know any other words. Every move Sasha had made had been "lovely" according to some social worker or other.

"They live about 80 miles away."

"In the country?" Sasha asked.

"No. In a city. But they've got a park close by."

"A city!" Sasha felt her anger start to rise. "There aren't any horses in cities."

Fran sighed. "I know there aren't. But I've already told you that I couldn't guarantee you could go on riding."

Sasha folded her arms defiantly and scowled. "Then I'm not going. I want to stay here." She turned to Joe and Beth, her eyes pleading with them to back her up.

But they didn't.

"We like you a lot," said Beth. "But you only came here for a little while." She reached out to touch Sasha's hand, but Sasha pulled it away like she always did. "This is too good a chance to turn down. Think about it – no more moves, no more changing school."

"No more horses," Sasha growled.

"Only for a while," said Joe. "You'll ride again one day – I'm sure you will. Maybe when you're grown up."

"I don't want to wait that long." Sasha felt like screaming in frustration.

At that point, Joe and Beth muttered something about having work to do and went outside. Sasha suspected their exit was pre-arranged to give her time alone with Fran, but she couldn't be sure. And what did it matter anyway? She hadn't changed their minds. They were just as bad as everyone else. They didn't want her.

Fran moved to the spare chair next to Sasha and opened the photo album to the first page. Then she pushed it in front of Sasha and leaned over to point at the people in the picture. "That's Sue and Tom," she announced.

Sasha didn't like her being so close. But she wanted the session to end as fast as possible, and the best way to make that happen was to stop arguing and co-operate. She shuffled sideways until she was balanced on the edge of her chair, as far away from Fran as she could get. Then she forced herself to look at the photo.

Sue and Tom looked a pretty ordinary couple. Ordinary clothes. Ordinary hair. Ordinary faces. There was nothing about them she could pick on as a reason not to live with them. Nothing except the lack of horses.

Fran kept up a running commentary as she turned the pages of the album, showing the rest of this very ordinary couple's very ordinary life. There was their house (lovely) and their car (lovely) and Tom's mum, who was looking forward to being a grandma.

Sasha sat in silence, barely listening as Fran's words washed over her. She could remember this stage of the introduction to Georgina and Gerald. It had been a different social worker then, but she'd been just as sure that everything was going to be perfect. Even Cynthia was supposed to be lovely. At least this new couple didn't have any children of their own.

It was a huge relief when Fran finally decided to go. "I'll bring Sue and Tom to meet you on Friday," she said as she was leaving. "I'm sure you're going to like them."

Sasha was less convinced, but she could see no point in arguing. Her opinion didn't matter. No one cared what she thought. She could hardly believe that a day that had started so wonderfully with her first gallop had ended with her whole world turned upside down.

As she watched Fran drive away, Sasha felt a knot of sorrow growing deep inside her chest. Hoping to keep the grief at bay by staying busy, she decided to feed Meteor early.

The bay horse looked calm again now, showing no sign of how terrified he had been earlier. But Sasha was still angry with herself for failing to catch him. She shoved his bowl under the fence and shook the hay out more forcefully than she needed to.

She left Meteor alone to eat and mooched around the farm for a while, unwilling to face Joe and Beth again. But eventually she heard Beth calling her for supper and knew she couldn't put it off any longer.

Joe smiled at her as she sat down at the table. "So what are these new people like? I hope they're not little green men from Mars."

Sasha gave a weak smile, pleased that he'd remembered what she'd said when she first saw that awful advert. "They're just ordinary," she replied, with a shrug. She shoved the photo album across the table. "You can look if you like."

Beth reached over and picked it up. "They look nice," she said, as she flicked through the pages. "I'm sure you'll like it there."

"I'm sure I won't," said Sasha, pushing her pasta around on her plate. The knot of sorrow in her chest had spread to her stomach, and she didn't feel like eating. "I don't want to go."

"We know," said Joe. "You must be tired of moving. But this will be the last time. Fran's sure of that."

"That's what they always say."

Beth put down her fork and looked at Sasha, her eyes full of sympathy. "I'm sure you'll be okay. Carl and Eddie were frightened too when they were told about their new families. But they're really happy with them now."

"I won't be," Sasha snapped. "I'll never be happy without horses." She threw down her fork. Anger was mixing with the sorrow now, threatening to make her lose control. How could they not understand?

She jumped to her feet, her eyes pricking with tears. She didn't want to cry now – not here in front of Joe and Beth. Crying showed how vulnerable she was – it was only safe to do that when she was completely alone.

"Sit down," said Beth gently.

"No! Leave me alone. I need to think." She ran towards the hall, heading for the stairs. Then she stopped. Her bedroom wasn't private enough. Beth might barge in like she did before. Right now, Sasha needed to be somewhere they didn't know – somewhere they would never find her. And she knew exactly the right place.

She raced outside, slammed the back door behind her and ran towards the bushes beside Meteor's field. The sun was low in the sky now and the shadows were long, but it wouldn't have mattered if it had been completely dark. She knew the way to her secret place so well that she could have found it with her eyes shut.

As she reached the tiny clearing beside the fence, the branches closed behind her and she was finally alone. There wasn't another human in sight – only Meteor far away on the other side of the field. He watched her climb up and sit on the top rail as usual. Then he went back to grazing, more interested in the grass than he was in her.

Now she was safe, she didn't have to pretend any longer. She put her head in her hands and let the tears come, her body shaking with silent sobs as the knot of grief inside her exploded, ballooned out and engulfed her.

She was so wrapped up in her own sorrow that she was barely aware of her surroundings. So she didn't realise she was no longer alone until she felt a draught of warm, gentle breath on her face. She glanced up and, through her tears, she saw the face of the bay horse close to hers.

Instinctively and without any fear, she reached out and touched his neck. He stood without flinching, letting her fingers caress his soft coat. The warmth of his body was reassuring.

Without thinking, she slid down on his side of the fence so she was standing beside him. She wasn't scared of him any more – it was as if he'd invited her into his world. Still crying, she slipped her hands around his neck and hugged him.

Meteor turned his head towards her, bending his neck around her body as if he was hugging her back. Comforted by his closeness, Sasha buried her face in his mane and wept as if her heart would break. And as she sobbed, the bay horse sighed deeply. It was as if she was crying for them both.

Chapter 19

By the time Sasha's tears finally died away, the sun had nearly vanished below the horizon, streaking the sky with dramatic shades of red and orange. She couldn't stay out here all night – she had to go back to the house soon. But she was reluctant to leave the comforting presence of the horse.

She ran her hands over his neck and face, stroking and caressing him. He nuzzled into her without pushing, seeming as keen as she was for them to stay together. Then she whispered a quiet goodbye and walked reluctantly across the field towards the yard. There seemed no point in going the long way around through the bushes now Meteor was happy to have her with him.

But the horse wasn't content to be left behind. He whickered gently and walked beside her, matching his speed with hers. Sasha reached up and rested her hand on his mane, thrilled that he was choosing to be with her. He seemed a totally different animal from the one that had terrified her on her first day.

When they reached the fence, Sasha stroked his face again and kissed him lightly. Then they finally had to part, and she walked back to the house alone, hardly daring to believe what had just happened.

She searched her pockets unsuccessfully for a tissue and wiped her eyes and nose with the bottom of her T-shirt instead. That was the best she could do. Maybe Joe and Beth wouldn't notice she'd been crying if she went straight up to her room.

They were both sitting at the kitchen table when she went inside. "Feeling better?" asked Joe.

"Sort of," said Sasha, staring at the floor so they couldn't see her face. She didn't want to share what had happened in the field. That was private between her and Meteor. So she muttered something about being tired and headed for her room.

"I put your album by your bed," Beth called after her.

Sasha didn't care where it was. She'd be happier if she never saw it again. And she didn't want to think about moving right now. Her mind was full of those magical moments with Meteor, and she didn't want to do anything to push away those memories.

Exhausted by the emotions of the day, Sasha slept better than she'd expected. When she woke in the morning, she wondered if she'd dreamed the whole thing. But the photo album on her bedside table was real enough. That proved Fran's visit was real and so were Sue and Tom Weaver.

Which just left Meteor. Surely she'd imagined that. Surely his behaviour couldn't have changed so dramatically and unexpectedly. And even if it had, did that mean the change was permanent or would he be back to his nervous self today?

There was only one way to find out. Sasha threw on her clothes and rushed out to the barn. Then she headed for his field, carrying his feed bowl in one hand and his hay tucked under the other arm.

Meteor was grazing on the far side as usual. He raised his head when he heard her coming as usual. Then he whinnied loudly and galloped across the grass – not running away as he'd done so many times before, but racing towards her with his black mane and tail streaming behind him. Sasha was sure she'd never seen him look so beautiful.

He skidded to a halt by the fence, exactly at the spot where she always fed him. He pawed at the ground impatiently until she reached him. Then he put his head over the fence and blew down his nose, whickering a gentle greeting.

Sasha smiled and stroked his face. Meteor's presence was just as warm and comforting as it had been the evening before. She pushed the bowl under the fence and sighed with contentment as he buried his nose in his feed. It was the first time he'd trusted her enough to eat with her beside him. And it felt so right, so perfect – as if they were meant to be together.

Moving home was going to be even harder now. She couldn't bear the thought of leaving Meteor forever. If only she'd succeeded in catching him yesterday, everything might be different now.

That's when she realised it wasn't too late. There was still time to show Beth and Joe what she'd done. And that might be enough to make them change their minds about keeping her. She ran and fetched a headcollar from the tack room. Then she headed for the house.

"Come quickly," she yelled, as she ran into the kitchen. "There's something you've got to see."

Joe laughed. "Judging by the grin on your face, it must be something good."

"It is," said Sasha. She hopped impatiently from foot to foot while they put on their boots. Then she hurried them towards Meteor's field.

He'd finished his feed now and was standing quietly munching his hay. But he paused when he saw Sasha coming and whinnied a welcome.

"That's good," said Joe. "He's not running away."

"That's just the beginning," said Sasha. "Watch this."

She handed Joe the headcollar, walked over to Meteor and stroked his face. Then she climbed over the fence and stood beside him, scratching his withers with her fingers.

"Wow!" said Beth. "How did you manage that?"

Sasha shrugged. "I don't know. He just came over." She didn't want to tell them about last night's tears. That was a secret only Meteor would ever know.

Joe looked at her sceptically, as if he suspected she was keeping something secret. "Maybe it's because you've changed," he suggested. "You don't seem scared of him any more."

"I'm not. I trust him completely."

"And he trusts you by the look of things," said Beth.

Sasha grinned. This was going well. "Give me the headcollar so I can catch him properly."

Joe looked doubtful. "I don't think that's a good idea. It might be asking too much of him too soon."

"But I'm sure I can do it," Sasha argued. "Look how calm he is." She stroked Meteor's head and ears to prove her point.

"He is very relaxed," said Beth. "It might work."

"I suppose it's worth a try," Joe reluctantly agreed. But he didn't take the headcollar to Sasha. Instead he beckoned to her to come and fetch it. "It's better if Beth and I don't get too close yet. It's you he's decided to trust, not us."

Sasha felt a twinge of nerves as she took it. This was her last chance to impress Joe and Beth. Suppose she messed it up? Suppose Meteor didn't trust her enough yet? Letting her stroke him was one thing. Letting her restrict his head with straps was quite another.

She took a deep breath to calm herself and concentrated totally on the bay horse, pushing everything else out of her head. Then she climbed back into the field and walked towards him again.

Meteor stood still and watched her until she was just a metre away. Then he walked towards her, stopping with his head just beside her hand – the one that was holding the headcollar. Had he not noticed it or was he signalling to her he was willing to be caught?

Sasha resisted the temptation to grab hold of his mane. Instead she slowly lifted the headcollar and held it in both hands, as if she was about to put it on. But she didn't try to force it over his head. Instead, she paused to give him time to get used to this new development.

Meteor sniffed the straps. Then he lowered his head towards them as if he was telling her she could go ahead. Slowly and gently, Sasha slid the headcollar over his nose and buckled the strap behind his ears. Then she held the rope in one hand while she patted his neck with the other.

"That was good horsemanship," said Joe, still standing some distance from the fence.

"You've worked wonders with him," said Beth.

Sasha beamed. This was an even better reaction than she'd hoped for. She'd lived at Kingfishers long enough to learn that Joe and Beth never gave praise when it wasn't due. They must be really impressed to make comments like that.

"Let's see if he can cope with us too," said Joe. He and Beth stepped cautiously forward, heading towards the bay horse. Meteor spotted the movement immediately. He raised his head warily and took a step backwards.

Sasha didn't try to stop him with the rope because she didn't want him to feel trapped. Instead she stepped back with him and ran her hand down his neck. "It's all right," she said soothingly and was pleased to feel his muscles relaxing under her fingers.

"Good girl," said Joe, as he finally reached them. "You handled that just right."

"Shall I bring him out of the field?" Sasha asked.

Beth shook her head. "Just bring him over to the gate and let him go. He's made huge progress today – we don't want to spoil it by pushing him too hard."

"Come on," Sasha said to Meteor and stepped forwards without pulling on the rope. The bay horse walked with her willingly, matching his pace to hers just as he had the night before.

As soon as they reached the gate, Sasha unbuckled the headcollar and slipped it off his head. But Meteor didn't leave. He stood beside her, totally relaxed, and rested his head against her arm.

Joe opened the gate. "That's enough for now," he said as he beckoned her through.

Sasha gave Meteor one last stroke. Then she stepped out of the field and joined Beth and Joe. "Did you mean what you said? Was that really good horsemanship?"

Joe nodded. "You know me. I never say what I don't mean."

"You've done really well," said Beth. "You should be proud of yourself."

Sasha hesitated, hardly daring to ask the question. But there might never be another moment as good as this. She had to take the risk. "Am I useful enough to stay?" she asked.

Joe looked totally confused. "What do you mean?"

"Being useful and staying don't go together," added Beth.

"Yes, they do. You told me so. You said you were keeping Calypso because he's useful."

"But he's a horse," said Beth. "It's not the same."

"Yes, it is," Sasha insisted. "The horses come and go and so do your foster children. But the useful horses stay and so can I if I'm useful enough."

"Oh, Sasha! It's not that simple." Beth reached out to hug her, but sighed and dropped her hands when Sasha ducked away. "We're not letting you go because you're not useful. We're doing it because you need a home where you can stay forever."

"But why can't that be here?"

Beth glanced away as if she was avoiding looking Sasha in the eye. "It just can't be. That's all."

"I'm sorry, Sasha," added Joe. "You've just got to accept that that's the way it is."

Sasha stared at them for a moment, hardly believing what she was hearing. Then she flung the headcollar down at their feet and, without another word, she thrust her hands deep into the pockets of her jeans and stomped away.

She didn't stop until she reached her secret place. As she climbed onto her usual spot on the fence, she felt angry and stupid and completely rejected. How could she have misjudged the situation so badly? Being useful hadn't made a scrap of difference – she'd wasted her time.

Then Meteor cantered up to her, and she realised she was wrong. She hadn't wasted a single minute she'd spent with this beautiful horse. They'd learned to trust each other in a way she had never trusted anyone before. And now she couldn't bear the thought of leaving him.

She buried her face in his mane, trying to fight back the wave of despair that threatened to engulf her. And all the time, Joe and Beth's words kept running through her head like a recording that had got stuck. "It just can't be. That's all." "You've just got to accept that that's the way it is."

But Sasha wasn't willing to accept anything that involved her leaving Kingfishers. Not without knowing the reason why she couldn't stay. Why were Joe and Beth so reluctant to tell her what that was?

Chapter 20

Meteor nuzzled Sasha's hand and gazed at her with brown eyes full of trust. His confidence in her helped replace her despair with determination. She couldn't give up now. She had to find a way to stay at Kingfishers with this wonderful horse.

She had no idea how to do that, but she was certain of one thing – for the time being, she wouldn't say any more about staying unless Joe and Beth brought up the subject. There was no point in irritating them. It wouldn't do any good, and it might even make things worse. Right now, it was far more important to keep her eyes and ears open for useful information. It might be easier to persuade Joe and Beth to change their minds if she knew the reason why they wouldn't keep her.

So when she finally went back to the house, she acted as if everything was fine. Joe and Beth glanced at each other in what she guessed was relief and followed her lead. And, despite the momentous events looming on the horizon, life at Kingfishers went back to normal.

For Sasha, that meant the rest of the morning spent on schoolwork with Beth and a riding lesson on Pumpkin in the afternoon. Thanks to Joe's careful teaching, she'd come a long way since she arrived and was just starting to jump.

When the lesson was over, she brushed the chestnut pony and turned him out to graze. Then she fetched Meteor's feed from the barn and set off to take it to him in his field. The bay horse saw her coming and cantered over to the fence to meet her.

But Joe stopped her before she reached him and took the feed bowl from her hands. "Try bringing him into the yard for this," he said, handing her a headcollar instead. "He'll be less worried about leaving his field if he knows there'll be food waiting for him."

Meteor was obviously surprised by the change in routine. He pricked his ears forward and neighed when he saw Joe carry his bowl away.

"It's okay," said Sasha, as she climbed through the fence. She walked over to Meteor and stroked his face. He gave her a welcoming nuzzle and stood quietly while she put the headcollar on him. Then he fell into step beside her as she walked calmly towards the gate.

It was only as she swung the gate open that Sasha felt a twinge of uneasiness. This field had been Meteor's home ever since he'd arrived. He was happy walking with her inside it, but how would he react when he got outside? Would he run away like he had that first day when he had raced out of the horsebox? Remembering his galloping hooves hurtling towards her made her stomach knot with nerves.

Meteor tensed too, staring apprehensively at the world beyond the gate. Sasha noticed the change in him and tightened her grip on the rope in case of trouble. Her heart started to race, and she found it hard to breathe. At almost exactly the same moment, Meteor snorted with fright and took two rapid steps backwards.

That's when Sasha realised that his fear might be feeding off hers. Perhaps he trusted her so much that when she was scared, he was too. And if that was true, maybe the reverse was too. She put her hand on his neck, took a deep breath to steady her nerves and forced away the memory of nearly being trampled. Instead she made a picture in her head of what she wanted to happen next – Meteor walking happily beside her into the yard.

As she kept breathing slowly and deeply, the nervous knot in her stomach gradually unravelled. And as her muscles relaxed, so did his. She could feel the tension in his body disappearing under her fingertips.

When she was sure they were both calm again she stepped through the open gateway as confidently as she could. And, to her relief, Meteor followed without any hesitation. Sasha couldn't stop smiling as they walked together to where his feed was waiting in the yard. It was wonderful to know that he trusted her so much.

As soon as they reached his bowl, Meteor plunged his head into it and started eating. Sasha waited until she was sure he was settled. Then she slipped his rope through a loop of string attached to a ring on the wall.

"Just hold the end," said Joe, before she had time to tie a knot. "That way you can let go if he runs back so he doesn't feel trapped. We know he's had bad things happen to him in the past, and some of them may have made him frightened of being tied up."

But Meteor didn't seem scared at all. He just stood quietly and ate his food without making any attempt to escape. Then he went calmly back to his field with Sasha.

He was just as relaxed when she brought him into the yard for his feed the next morning. So, after he had finished his breakfast, Sasha tentatively tied him up with a quick release knot and walked over to the tack room. Meteor watched her go, but didn't try to follow her. He seemed to know he was supposed to stay where he was.

She fetched a grooming kit and set to work on his coat, using a rubber curry comb to loosen the layers of dirt that had built up during long months of neglect. Then she switched to a soft bristled brush that sent clouds of loose hair, mud and dust tumbling to the ground.

After she'd brushed him all over, she stepped back and looked at the result with satisfaction. Meteor's mahogany brown coat was still a long way from perfect, but it was much cleaner. There were already places where it gleamed in the sunlight, making him look more beautiful than ever.

Sasha changed brushes again and turned her attention to his long black tail, teasing out the tangles with her fingers so as not to hurt him. She was only part way through when Joe came over.

He looked at Meteor and nodded approvingly. "That's a huge improvement, but it's probably enough for today. Why don't you take him for a walk around the farm?"

Sasha was thrilled. "Do you mean I can ride him?"

"Absolutely not," said Joe, shaking his head. "Meteor's made good progress, but it'll be ages before he's ready for riding. Just walk him around on the lead rope so he gets to know the place and the other horses. It will help build up his confidence."

Sasha felt a wave of disappointment wash over her. *Ages* sounded like such a long time – much longer than she had left at Kingfishers. And, if it was, leading Meteor was the most she would ever be able to do. She'd have to leave without ever sitting on his back.

She undid the rope and led Meteor away from the yard. He walked confidently beside her with his head level with her shoulder and his pace matched perfectly to hers. She reached out and touched his face. His hair felt silky soft under her fingers.

They turned through an open gateway and set off across an empty field, just the two of them alone in the quietness of the countryside. It was like the closeness they'd shared on the night she'd cried. Although Sasha still longed to jump on his back and ride him, walking together like this was definitely the next best thing.

For the rest of the week, their outings together were the high spots of every day. She felt safe with Meteor, able to stop pretending and be herself. While they ambled through the fields together, she found herself sharing things with him that she'd never told another living soul. How happy she'd felt when Mum was her normal self and how frightened she'd been when she wasn't. How the smell of alcohol and the sound of angry voices brought back memories she would rather forget. And how she hated always being an outsider and never belonging anywhere.

Meteor always stayed extra close when she was talking like that. Sometimes he'd rest his head against her arm and sigh – not pushing or rubbing, just being her friend. Sometimes he'd toss his head and suggest they went for a run to clear their minds. Then he'd trot beside her as she raced across the grass and the bad memories would fly away, leaving her laughing with sheer pleasure.

She wished those few days could last forever. But Friday arrived, whether she wanted it to or not, and with it came Fran and Sue and Tom.

Chapter 21

Sasha's heart pounded as she watched Fran's car drive up to the house. This was it. Another move, another start with strangers. Why couldn't she be like other kids and stay in one place? More to the point, why couldn't she stay here?

She stood a few paces behind Joe and Beth, watching apprehensively as the visitors climbed out of Fran's car. Overhead, grey clouds filled the sky, their sombre colouring a perfect match for Sasha's mood.

She recognised Sue and Tom easily from their photos. Sue was short and dumpy with perfectly styled hair. Thanks to the red trousers and red top she was wearing, she reminded Sasha of a huge tomato. Tom was taller, thin as a beanpole and much less flamboyant. His clothes were boring browns and his hair was cropped short – what there was of it. He was well on his way to being completely bald.

Sue waved and gave a nervous smile. "You must be Sasha."

Sasha nodded and shrank further away. She wasn't ready to meet them yet, and she wasn't sure she ever would be.

Beth filled the silence before it became awkward. "Come in and have a coffee. Sasha and I have baked a cake specially."

As they walked towards the house, Fran waved her hand at the surrounding countryside. "I told you it was lovely here."

"But it's so remote," said Tom. "There's nothing but fields."

What else would you expect on a farm? thought Sasha. But she didn't say anything.

"It must be hard being so far from the shops," gushed Sue, when they'd sat down at the kitchen table. She looked directly at Sasha and added, "I love shopping. Don't you?"

Sasha gave a non-committal shrug. Then she realised everyone was looking at her, expecting her to say something. "It depends. Supermarkets are boring, but tack shops are okay." She'd enjoyed the one she'd visited with Beth the previous week.

Sue's eyebrows rose questioningly. "Tack shops. What are they?"

Sasha stifled a groan. It was true. These people knew nothing about horses. "Tack shops sell tack," she stated bluntly, making no attempt to hide her exasperation.

"Saddles and bridles and things like that," Joe explained.

There was an awkward pause. This time Beth dealt with it by producing the coffee. As they'd already arranged, Sasha fetched the cake and served everyone a generous slice.

"Lemon drizzle. My favourite," said Sue. She patted her ample hips. "I shouldn't really, but I can't resist."

Tom laughed. "You can see I don't have the same problem. I never put on weight however much I eat. Sue says I've got hollow legs."

This comment triggered a conversation between the adults on weight watching and the merits of different diets. Sasha was glad she wasn't expected to join in. Her mouth was so dry with fear that it was difficult to eat her cake. But she nibbled at it anyway while she stole wary glances at Sue and Tom.

They seemed pleasant enough, but she wished they weren't here. If only they'd never seen that advert. If only they'd found some other girl to take into their home instead of her. Everything was going so well until they appeared.

"Why don't you take Sue and Tom up to your bedroom?" Fran suggested when they'd finished eating. Although she phrased it as a question, the tone of her voice made it sound more like an order.

Sasha glared at her. She didn't want these strangers nosing through her things. "I'd rather show them the horses," she said quickly. She'd feel safer outside, more relaxed away from the confines of the house and Fran's inquisitive eyes.

"That would be lovely," said Sue.

"We'll go and get our boots," Tom added. "Fran warned us to come prepared for country walking."

Sasha took them on exactly the same guided tour that she'd given to Fran weeks before. But Sue and Tom were much more enthusiastic than the social worker had been. They walked confidently, their boot-clad feet striding through the mud and manure without any hesitation. They enjoyed spotting wild rabbits and birds, and they seemed to genuinely like the horses, especially Pumpkin.

"He's such a sweetie," said Sue. "Round and orange – just like his name."

Sasha left Meteor until last, not sure if she wanted to share him with them at all. In the end, he made the decision for her by trotting to the fence when he saw them walking near his field. But he kept close to Sasha, watching the newcomers warily. "He's still nervous with strangers," she explained, as she stroked his nose. "He's moved about a lot."

"Just like you," said Tom. "But don't worry. We want this to be the last move you ever have to make. We're sure about that."

Sasha gave him full marks for trying. She just didn't believe him.

"And we're really glad you're coming to live with us," Sue added. "We've always wanted a daughter." She paused, obviously hoping Sasha would say something nice in response.

Sasha didn't oblige. She didn't want to pretend she was happy about leaving, and she couldn't see the point in telling them the truth. No one was listening to her. No one cared.

After an awkward gap, Tom changed the subject. "Fran's told us you're upset at stopping riding. So we've been looking at things you might like to do instead."

"There are some lovely dance classes round the corner," gushed Sue. "They do modern and jazz as well as ballet. And there's a swimming club at the leisure centre."

They don't understand. These people thought riding was just another hobby – one that was easy to replace. But nothing could ever take the place of the horses in her heart, not even a puppy or a kitten – and neither of those was even on offer.

"And, of course, there's lots of sport at your new school," Sue continued, oblivious to the distress her words were causing.

New school! The words filled Sasha with alarm. She'd been so busy worrying about leaving the horses that she'd forgotten all about school. After she'd moved, there'd be no more lessons with Beth. No more help to fill all those gaps in her learning. She'd be back to failing and being shouted at and everyone thinking she was stupid.

That's when the rain started. Just a few drops at first, but rapidly turning into a deluge. "My hair!" squeaked Sue, putting her hands over her head in a vain attempt to keep it dry.

"Run!" shouted Sasha, and she raced off towards the house with Sue and Tom close behind. The rain was even heavier now, pouring down her face and sticking her shirt to her back. It was a relief to finally reach the kitchen – dry, warm and full of familiar smells.

Sue and Tom ran in after her. Sue's face was so red from the unexpected exercise that it nearly matched her top, making her look more like a tomato than ever. Her once neat hair was plastered to her head, lank and straight without a sign of the curls she had arrived with.

"Oh dear," said Beth, handing out towels. "You'd better get those wet things off so I can dry them."

Sasha went up to her room to change, glad of the chance to be on her own. She took her time and delayed going back downstairs for as long as she could. When she eventually arrived, she found Sue and Tom wrapped in borrowed dressing gowns while the tumble dryer rumbled in the corner of the kitchen.

The rain was still streaming down the windows. "That's put an end to anything outdoors," said Joe.

"We could play a game," Beth suggested.

Sue beamed. "Have you got Scrabble? I love playing that."

Sasha didn't. It was all about words, and she had no desire to show these people how bad she was at spelling.

As usual, Beth understood without being told. "Monopoly's better for six," she said.

They spread the board on the floor in the living room and started playing. Sasha was glad that Beth and Joe joined in. It eased the atmosphere for her having people there she knew and, when she had to read, Beth gave her that "you can do it" look she used so much in lessons.

The game went on all afternoon, except for a break to allow Sue and Tom to get dressed in their dry clothes. Sasha played with a bold recklessness that combined with luck to get results. Her hotel on Mayfair knocked Fran out of the game first, swiftly followed by Sue and Beth.

Joe laughed and tossed down his last few remaining banknotes. "There's no point in prolonging the agony. I surrender."

"So do I," said Tom. He smiled at Sasha. "You're the champion for today."

Despite the smile, Sasha noticed he was more serious than Joe – less inclined to laugh. Or was that just the effect of being nervous? Maybe today was as difficult for him as it was for her.

Fran glanced at her watch. "I'm afraid we'll have to leave soon. We've got a long drive back. But we need to make some plans first." She opened her bag and pulled out her diary.

Sue gave an excited smile and exchanged glances with Tom. "We're hoping Sasha can come to live with us as soon as possible."

"There doesn't seem any point in hanging around," added Tom.

"I agree," said Fran.

"I don't," said Sasha. Everything was happening too fast. She wanted it to slow down – to give her more time with Meteor. More time to find out why Joe and Beth wouldn't keep her. And more time to make them change their minds.

Sue and Tom looked disappointed. But Beth sprang to her defence. "This is a big step for Sasha. It's only natural that she's scared."

"Of course, it is," Fran agreed. She opened her diary and thumbed through the pages. Then she looked up and smiled at Sasha. "I'll take you to visit your new home on Sunday. I'm sure you'll feel less frightened when you've seen where you are going to live."

Joe raised his eyebrows. "I thought social workers didn't like working weekends."

"This one doesn't mind when it's something important." She looked at Sasha and smiled sympathetically. "My instinct tells me that dragging this move out isn't going to help you at all. So we might as well get it done quickly."

"When's it going to happen?" asked Tom. "It would be good to have a date so I can book some time off work to help Sasha settle in."

Fran flicked through her diary. "How about Tuesday?"

Sue beamed, her eyes shining with anticipation. "That will be perfect."

Tuesday! Sasha didn't argue. There wasn't any point when no one was listening to her. But her heart was pounding, and the palms of her hands were damp with panic. It was already Friday. She only had four days left at Kingfishers. Four days before she had to say goodbye to Meteor forever.

Chapter 22

Sasha was relieved when her visitors finally drove away. She refused all Joe and Beth's attempts to talk about how she felt and tried to go on as if nothing had happened. But deep inside she knew she was only pretending. Everything was different now. The clock was ticking, and this happy interlude in her life would soon be over. A new school, a new home, new foster parents. And no horses! Nothing would ever be the same again.

She was so wrapped up in her own thoughts that she barely noticed the phone ring or Beth run to take the call in the office. It was only when she bounced back into the kitchen, her face wreathed in smiles, that Sasha realised something had happened.

Beth gave Joe an excited hug. "That was Dawn. She's coming home for the weekend."

Joe grinned. "Brilliant. It's ages since we last saw her."

Sasha had never seen either of them so happy before. And suddenly everything that was happening made sense. Dawn must be the reason she couldn't stay. Joe and Beth already had a daughter, and she didn't want a sister.

Beth turned to her. "Dawn's looking forward to meeting you. She's a lovely girl. I'm sure you'll like her."

Sasha gave a non-committal shrug. Beth obviously thought her daughter was an angel. But Sasha was sure she wasn't. Dawn would be like Cynthia – resenting her presence in her home and treating her like an intruder. That must be why she was coming now – to make sure Sasha really was going to leave.

She slunk upstairs, eager to be alone. The house had changed since the day she first arrived. The repair work was finished, the clutter on the landing had gone and the air was filled with the fresh scent of paint. The bedroom Zack had set on fire was freshly decorated now and ready to use. But Sasha had chosen to stay in the box room with the dancing teddies on the walls. There was already too much change in her life – she couldn't face any more.

The room felt cosy and familiar now – even the bears seemed welcoming. She slumped on the bed, picked up the photo album and started thumbing through the pages. The photos told her more now she'd met Sue and Tom. Perhaps life with them wouldn't be too bad. Better than Georgina and Gerald's anyway. But even if it wasn't, she still had to go there. She still had to leave Kingfishers and she still had to say goodbye to Meteor forever.

It was so unfair! And it was all Dawn's fault!

Sasha exploded with anger and hurled the album away as hard as she could. It soared across the room and thudded harmlessly into the wardrobe. But on the way, it clipped the corner of Mum's photo frame and sent it crashing to the ground.

The sound of breaking glass brought Sasha to her senses. She knelt on the wooden floor and lifted the frame carefully. It was smashed beyond repair, but thankfully the photograph itself was undamaged. Mum still held baby Sasha close. Mum still smiled at the camera instead of staring vaguely into the distance like she did after everything went wrong.

Sasha wrapped the big bits of broken glass in a tissue and put them in the bin. Then she took another tissue and brushed the smaller bits down the gaps between the floorboards where they couldn't cut her feet. Finally, she perched the damaged frame back on her bedside table. Although the photo was no longer protected, she still wanted to be able to see it.

She took one last look at the reminder of happier times. Then she climbed into bed, buried her head in her pillow and silently cried herself to sleep.

The next morning, the kitchen smelt delicious. Beth bubbled with excitement as she cooked and chopped and stirred. "We're having lasagne," she explained, when Sasha came back from feeding Meteor. "That's

Dawn's favourite. And apple crumble with custard. That's her favourite too. And I thought I'd make a coffee cake. She loves that."

Dawn, Dawn, Dawn. She hadn't even arrived yet, and Sasha was already sick of her. She slipped out of the house, determined not to be there when the source of all her problems turned up. She fetched Meteor and set off on one of their walks together, but her curiosity soon got the better of her so she stopped and let him graze in a place with a good view of the house. From here, she could watch Dawn's arrival from a safe distance.

She didn't have to wait long. After only a few minutes, a small, red car drove up the lane and parked. A young woman climbed out of the driver's side. But before Sasha could see what she looked like, she was swamped by Joe and Beth both hugging her at the same time.

Sasha was surprised how jealous she felt as she watched Dawn hug them back and heard their laughter carried towards her on the breeze. She envied them their closeness, their ability to let themselves touch and be touched without the fear that was so ingrained in her.

"Come on," she said to Meteor and turned away. She'd seen enough. She didn't want to watch any more. The bay horse took one last mouthful of grass and followed her.

When they reached the yard, she was pleased to find they were the only ones there. She tied Meteor in his usual spot and fetched her grooming kit. She brushed his mahogany brown coat until it gleamed in the sunlight. Then she picked up the end of his black tail and started work on the tangles. She was so intent on her task that she didn't notice the footsteps behind her. So the voice that belonged to them made her jump.

"What a beautiful horse!"

Sasha swung round and saw a young woman looking at her with grey-blue eyes that were startlingly like Joe's. She had his long, lanky build too, although she wasn't quite as tall, and her curly hair was exactly like Beth's. Even if Sasha had never seen the photo on the piano, she would have no trouble recognising who she was. There was no doubt about it. She was definitely Joe and Beth's daughter.

"Hello, Sasha. Mum and Dad said you'd probably be up here."

Sasha felt a fresh twinge of jealousy at the easy way Dawn referred to Joe and Beth as Mum and Dad. She rolled the words around in her head, wondering what it would be like to say them herself. It was such a long time since she'd called anyone "Mum" and there had never been a real dad in her life – just a succession of Mum's boyfriends, some of whom she'd prefer to forget.

Dawn smiled and held out her hand. "I'm Dawn, by the way."

"I guessed," said Sasha. She ignored the outstretched hand and stepped away so she was standing on the other side of Meteor, holding his tail between them like a barrier.

"And I guess this must be Meteor. I've heard what a fantastic job you've done with him."

The compliment made Sasha open up a little. "He's the best horse in the world. He just needed time to realise it."

Dawn walked gently towards the bay horse and ran her hand along his neck. Sasha hoped he would reject this newcomer and refuse all contact with her. But he didn't. Instead he stood quietly and allowed Dawn to stroke his face.

Sasha was surprised and disappointed. Why wasn't he as wary of this new arrival as she was? Could he sense that she was safe to be near? And, if so, should Sasha follow his lead?

Dawn grinned. "I'm going out on a hack this afternoon. Do you want to come with me on Meteor?"

Sasha wished she could. She longed to get on the bay horse's back and feel his powerful muscles moving underneath her. But she shook her head. "I can't. Joe says Meteor's not ready to ride yet."

"That's a shame," said Dawn. "But it doesn't matter. You can use Pumpkin instead."

"Don't you mind? He's yours."

"And he's much too small for me. I'm going to ride Calypso, so Pumpkin will just be sitting around getting fatter if you don't make him do some work."

Sasha still didn't trust Dawn, and she wasn't at all sure she wanted to spend time with her. But the chance of a ride in the countryside was too good to miss. She might not get another one for a very long time. "Okay," she agreed quietly, hoping she wouldn't regret her decision.

Chapter 23

It felt strange having an extra person at the table for lunch. Sasha stared at her plate in silence and pushed her lasagne around with her fork. It wasn't just Dawn's favourite. It was hers too. But today she didn't feel hungry. Watching Dawn with Joe and Beth made her painfully aware that she was an outsider. No wonder she couldn't stay. This was Dawn's home and Dawn's family – not hers.

Thoughtful as always, Beth tried to draw her into the conversation. "Have you two decided where you're going this afternoon?" she asked.

Sasha shook her head. "I like Buckberry Ridge," she suggested.

"That's not far enough," said Dawn. "Let's go up Kite Hill. I love the view from the top."

"Great," said Sasha with real enthusiasm. She fancied riding somewhere she hadn't been before. But even if she hadn't, she would have said "yes" anyway. She had no desire to disagree with Dawn. Disagreeing with Cynthia had always landed her in trouble.

For the rest of the meal, Dawn entertained them with funny stories about training to be a vet. And as she listened, Sasha found herself laughing along with the others. Perhaps she wasn't as much of an outsider as she'd thought.

Dawn's ready smile and bubbly sense of humour were very different from grumpy Cynthia and her perpetual scowl. She seemed warm and friendly instead of spiteful and, surprisingly, there was no sign that she resented Sasha being there.

Despite this, Sasha was cautious when they finally went to the yard. She worked slowly and carefully as she groomed and saddled Pumpkin. He was Dawn's pony. She didn't want to annoy her by making mistakes.

"Okay, let's go," said Dawn, when both horses were ready. She put her foot in the stirrup and leapt onto Calypso's saddle as effortlessly as Joe always did. "Come on. Your turn."

Sasha felt clunky and awkward in comparison as she swung herself onto Pumpkin's back and settled herself in the saddle, trying to sit exactly as Joe had taught her. She wished Dawn wasn't watching. It made her nervous, as if this was some kind of test. She picked up the reins with hands that were suddenly all thumbs and squeezed her legs against the pony's sides. To her relief, Pumpkin stepped forward obediently and clattered out of the yard beside Calypso.

It was a perfect afternoon for a ride – clear and sunny with enough breeze to stop the horses getting too hot, but not so much that it made them spooky. Dawn was as warm and friendly as she had been during the meal. She chattered to Sasha as they rode side by side and made no attempt to criticise the way she was handling Pumpkin.

That helped Sasha to relax and, as her nervousness disappeared, she started to enjoy herself. She pushed away the thought that she might never be able to go on a ride like this again and concentrated on making the most of every moment.

When they reached the river, they discovered they weren't the only ones enjoying the good weather. "Look! There's a kingfisher," said Dawn, pointing at a flash of blue wings darting down towards the water.

"That's the first one I've seen," said Sasha. "I never realised they were so small."

"Maybe that's why you didn't spot them before," said Dawn. "There are always kingfishers here."

"Is that how the farm got its name?" Sasha asked.

Dawn shrugged. "I don't know. It was already called that when we came here. I was only six then, and I used to pretend there were fairies down here by the river."

"I'd rather have fairies than these flies," said Sasha, as they rode into a cloud of midges lurking in the shadows. Pumpkin didn't like them either. He tossed his head to stop them landing on his face.

There were fewer flies when they turned uphill onto a path through a wood, but there was plenty of other wildlife. Sasha was the first to spot the squirrel scurrying up the trunk of a tall pine and the woodpecker high in its branches. But she didn't see the pheasant until it shot out of a low bush, right under Pumpkin's nose.

He jumped sideways in surprise and tried to spin round. But Sasha stopped him just in time and closed her legs against his side, urging him forward again. Pumpkin hesitated for a moment, snorting at the hedge in suspicion in case it was hiding another bird. Then he walked on as if nothing had happened.

"Well done," said Dawn. "You stayed really calm."

"I didn't feel it. That bird made me jump too." Sasha surprised herself with her own honesty. She wouldn't have told Fran or Sue or Tom how she felt.

Dawn laughed. "Well, it didn't show and that's all that matters. You're a good rider."

Her praise made Sasha glow with pride. Now she knew her better, she was glad Dawn had chosen this particular weekend to visit. Although she was technically grown up, she was only eight years older than Sasha and fun to be with.

They rode on together through the wood, sometimes walking, sometimes trotting and occasionally breaking into a canter. Much to Sasha's delight, Dawn even found them some logs to jump. Pumpkin cleared them with enthusiasm. He seemed to be enjoying himself as much as Sasha was.

At last, they came out into the sunlight again on a wide grassy path that stretched away up Kite Hill, between occasional patches of gorse. Pumpkin saw the open space ahead and tugged at the reins, eager to go faster. Sasha shared his excitement. "It's the perfect place for a gallop," she said.

Dawn grinned. "That's just what I was thinking." She urged Calypso forward, and Sasha did the same with Pumpkin.

The two horses leapt forward and raced side by side up the hill. Sasha bent low over Pumpkin's neck as his hooves thundered across the grass and the wind whipped through his mane. She was loving every minute of this ride.

They let the horses gallop for as long as they wanted. But eventually the slight slope and Pumpkin's fat tummy sapped his energy. He slowed to a canter, then a trot. Dawn let Calypso do the same. Although his legs were longer, he was tired too.

They gave the horses a long rein so they could stretch their necks. Then they ambled up the rest of the hill until they reached the top. "Let's stop and give them a rest," said Dawn.

They jumped off, ran up their stirrups and loosened their girths. Then they took the reins over the horses' heads and held them while they grazed. Calypso nibbled gently, stopping now and then to rest, while Pumpkin ate as fast as he could, biting off huge mouthfuls of grass.

Dawn laughed at him. "No wonder he's so fat. He never stops eating."

"Except when he's asleep," added Sasha. Now they'd stopped riding, she could look at the view properly for the first time. It was fantastic. She could see for miles.

"Look! There's Kingfishers," said Dawn, pointing down to her right.

"Doesn't it look tiny," said Sasha. "I love it up here." Then she turned to Dawn and added, "Thanks for letting me come with you."

"You don't have to thank me. I'm enjoying your company."

"Really?" said Sasha.

"Of course. I've always hoped Mum and Dad would foster a girl. The boys were all right, but it's more fun having you around – like having a little sister." She stopped and stared silently into the distance for a few seconds. Then she whispered, "I had a sister once, a long time ago."

"I know," Sasha whispered back. "Her picture's on the piano."

Dawn picked a leaf from a nearby bush and rolled it between her fingertips. "Has Mum told you much about her?"

"Only that her name was Jennifer, and she died."

"So you don't know she was born the same year as you. If she were still alive, you'd be exactly the same age."

Sasha was too stunned to speak. Was this the reason why Joe and Beth didn't want her to stay? Did Sasha seem like a ghost from the past – a second-rate substitute for the daughter who died? The more she thought about it, the more convinced she was that she was right. She couldn't be part of Joe and Beth's family because they didn't want her to take the place reserved for their lost baby.

Suddenly Dawn broke the silence. "Look!" she cried, as she pointed at the sky. "It's a kite – a red kite."

Sasha stared up and saw a bird soaring overhead. It was riding the air currents with outstretched wings, gliding slowly as it hunted for prey. "It's beautiful. Are you sure it's a kite?"

"Positive. I recognise the wing shape. We should both make a wish – it's supposed to be lucky to see a kite from Kite Hill."

"Wishes don't work." Sasha had learned that the hard way.

"But they're still fun." Dawn closed her eyes for a moment, then opened them again. "There. I've made mine. Now it's your turn."

Sasha closed her eyes and wished hard. *Let me stay at Kingfishers.* But even as she said the words silently in her head, she was sure they wouldn't come true. Joe and Beth wanted Jennifer – not her.

Chapter 24

The ride back was slower than the ride out, but it was just as enjoyable. Sasha was tired when they finally got back to Kingfishers. She'd never ridden so far before and, now she knew the truth about Jennifer, she doubted that she ever would again.

It was late by the time they had fed the horses and turned them out. They got back to the house just as Beth had finished cooking supper. It was delicious as always and, when they had finished eating, they sat on the floor in the living room and played Monopoly again

Sasha didn't win this time. But she enjoyed the game more than she had the day before. There was none of the awkwardness she'd felt with Sue and Tom and Fran. Being here with Dawn and Joe and Beth felt so right – as if she was part of a real family with a real sister and a real mum and dad. And just for the evening, she let herself pretend that was true.

When Joe finally won, Beth brought in the coffee cake. Dawn laughed when she saw it. "That's my wish come true," she said to Sasha. "I hope yours does too."

Sasha was too overwhelmed with sadness to speak. Remembering the wish had brought her fantasy crashing down around her ears. And, for the first time ever, she realised it wasn't just Meteor and the other horses she was going to miss. It was Joe and Beth and Dawn as well.

She didn't want any of them to realise how upset she was. So she gulped down the last of her cake and stood up. "I'm off to bed. Fran's picking me up early."

As soon as she reached her room, she changed into her pyjamas. But she was too tense to sleep so she sat cross-legged on her bed and turned the pages of the photo album. Sue and Tom smiled out at her. They looked more familiar now, but she still couldn't imagine living with them.

Her thoughts were interrupted by a gentle tap on the door. "Can I come in?" called Dawn. "I've made myself some hot chocolate and thought you might like some too."

"Okay," said Sasha. She wasn't sure she wanted company right now. But the hot chocolate was too tempting to resist.

The door swung slowly open and Dawn came in holding two mugs. She handed one to Sasha and held the other in both hands while she gazed around the room. "This place has been the junk store for so long that I've almost forgotten what it's like as a bedroom."

"I like it," said Sasha. "It's cosy."

"It's certainly small." Dawn walked over to the wall beside the window and ran her fingers across the dancing bears. "I still like this paper just as much as I did when I chose it."

"Was this your room then?" asked Sasha, curious about what had happened here in the past.

Dawn shook her head. "It was Jennifer's. Or it would have been if she'd ever come home from hospital." She gave a sad sigh and stroked the bears again. "Mum and Dad let me choose the wallpaper. They thought I'd be less jealous of the new baby if I was involved in getting everything ready for her. We put the same paper in both nurseries."

"Both?" said Sasha. "Why did she need two?"

"Because we had two homes." Dawn sat down on the bed beside Sasha and took a sip of her hot chocolate before she continued. "Everything was different then. Dad was an investment banker so we lived in the city most of the time to be near his job. But at weekends and holidays, we escaped to Kingfishers. So Jennifer needed a nursery in both places. Or we thought she would."

"What happened?" asked Sasha. She was suddenly keen to know more about these people who she liked so much.

Dawn smiled sadly as she remembered. "Jennifer was born with a very rare disease – one the doctors couldn't cure. She just got weaker and weaker until she died. That's when everything changed."

"What do you mean?"

"Mum cried all the time, and Dad was so upset that he couldn't work for ages. He lost his high-powered job and all the pay that went with it. So we left the city behind and moved to Kingfishers permanently. And gradually we discovered that working with horses helped us to understand ourselves better and heal our grief. That's when Mum and Dad decided to do it for a living."

Sasha wasn't sure what to say. It was hard to imagine Joe and Beth living anywhere other than Kingfishers. They seemed so settled – so much part of the place. And so were the horses.

Dawn smiled. "I've told you my story. Are you going to tell me yours?"

Sasha tensed, not sure she wanted to share anything about herself. "It's boring," she said, hoping that Dawn would lose interest.

She didn't. Instead she leaned forward and looked at the photo on Sasha's bedside table. "Is that your mum?" she asked.

Sasha nodded.

"She's pretty," said Dawn "It's a shame the glass is broken. What happened?"

"It fell over," said Sasha, without revealing her part in the accident.

"I've got a spare one in my cupboard. You can have it if you like." Without waiting for a reply, Dawn ran out of the room and returned a few minutes later clutching a smart new frame with a silver edge. "I think it's the right size," she said, as she pushed it into Sasha's hands.

She was right. Mum's photo fitted perfectly. "Thanks," said Sasha as she placed it back on the bedside table.

"Is your mum dead too? Like Jennifer."

Sasha shook her head. "She's still alive, but she's not very good at the mum thing. Social Services kept trying to get me back with her, but it never worked. She's more interested in drugs and drink and boyfriends than she is in me. And every time I had to leave again, I went to a different foster home. That's one of the reasons I've moved so much." She stopped, surprised by her own willingness to talk about the past. Maybe that was because Dawn had shared with her first, or maybe it was because she felt like a big sister.

"That must have been horrible," said Dawn. "What happened then?"

"Lots more moves," said Sasha. "I never seem to fit in anywhere. The last people were supposed to be adopting me, but that all went wrong too and I came here instead."

"I'm glad you did," said Dawn. "I wish you were staying."

Her words took Sasha by surprise. "I wish I was too. But Joe and Beth don't want me to." She couldn't bring herself to call them 'your mum and dad'. It felt too strange.

Dawn frowned. "That doesn't make sense. They've told me how much they like you."

Sasha was thrilled to hear that, but it made their decision even harder to accept. "I think it's because I'm the same age as Jennifer. They don't want me to take her place."

"That's rubbish!" said Dawn. "Jennifer's one of the reasons Mum and Dad started fostering in the first place. They wanted to fill the hole she left in their lives, and they wanted to use horses to help troubled kids in the same way they helped us."

Sasha felt even more confused than she had been before. "I don't understand. If you all like me and Jennifer's not a problem, why can't I stay?"

Dawn drank the last of her hot chocolate and gazed thoughtfully at the empty cup. "I don't know," she said. "But I'll ask if you like. Maybe I can make them change their minds."

Sasha almost bounced off the bed in excitement. "Can you do it now?" she begged. There was so little time left before she had to move.

Dawn shook her head. "It's too late tonight. But I promise I'll talk to them tomorrow before I go back to college." She stared at Sasha's doubtful expression and added, "Don't worry. I'm like Mum and Dad. I always keep my promises."

Sasha hoped she was telling the truth. She'd already tried everything else she could think of. Now she had to trust Dawn enough to let her help. It was the only chance she had left.

Chapter 25

The next morning was bright and sunny – a perfect day for riding. Sasha wished she could go for another hack with Dawn or take Meteor for a walk or do anything other than visit Sue and Tom. But there was no chance of that. She had to go.

Fran surprised everyone by arriving on time. As she drove up to the front of the house, Joe, Beth and Dawn went outside to meet her. Sasha followed reluctantly, her shoulders slumped in gloom.

Dawn turned and winked at her. "Don't worry," she whispered. "I haven't forgotten. I promise I'll do it."

Sasha straightened up a little and smiled back. Dawn's words had lifted her spirits, reminding her there was still a chance, however small, that the move might not happen. And that flicker of hope might help her cope with the difficult visit ahead.

Fran turned down Beth's usual offer of coffee. "Sorry. We haven't got time." Then she smiled at Sasha. "Jump in quickly. We've a long drive ahead."

"Have a lovely day," Joe said, as he held the car door open.

"We'll be thinking of you," added Beth. Then she spread her arms in yet another attempt to give Sasha a hug.

This time Sasha fought back her instinctive desire to step away. She'd felt so jealous when Beth hugged Dawn yesterday – it didn't make sense to avoid the same thing happening to her. But her body stiffened automatically as Beth's arms closed around her. She felt trapped, surrounded by the warmth and scent of this woman she'd never let so close before. Her heart was racing and she could hardly breathe as she stood completely still, too scared to hug Beth back or to take any pleasure from what was happening.

Then it was over as quickly as it had started. Sasha stepped away, relieved to be free. But she was confused too. Dawn had obviously enjoyed her hug yesterday. So why hadn't Sasha enjoyed this one?

Part of her wondered how Beth felt about it. The other part didn't want to know. So she avoided looking her foster mother in the eye as she climbed into the car and waved goodbye. "See you later," she called, trying to sound more cheerful than she felt. Today she was coming back. But, unless Dawn succeeded with Joe and Beth, Tuesday would be different. On Tuesday, she'd be leaving forever.

Sasha was pleased when Fran switched on the radio. She didn't share her social worker's choice in music, but listening to the classics meant neither of them had to talk. She stared through the side window and looked for horses, just as she had when she'd left Cynthia's house. That seemed a world away now – she felt so much part of Kingfishers.

The countryside rolled past, as they sped along the motorway. Then they turned off onto ordinary roads that were nearly as busy. Soon the green fields were replaced by street after street of almost identical houses with just a few trees struggling to survive amongst the traffic fumes. There were no horses to spot now so Sasha daydreamed about Meteor instead, imagining how wonderful it would be to ride the bay horse – to gallop him up Buckberry Ridge with his powerful muscles moving beneath her and his mane and tail streaming behind him in the wind.

Eventually Fran pulled up outside a neat house with a neat garden. It looked just like the pictures in the photo album. It was also just like all the other houses in the road. But it was completely different from the house at Kingfishers, and Sasha knew instantly which one she preferred.

Sue and Tom must have been looking out for them. They flung open the front door as soon as the car stopped and hurried down the drive, beaming with pleasure. The curls were back in Sue's hair now, lacquered so carefully into place that they didn't bounce at all when she moved. But other bits of her did – she was very plump – and Tom looked balder than ever.

Sasha climbed reluctantly out of the car and stood behind Fran, ready to duck any attempt to touch her. The unsuccessful hug from Beth had been quite enough closeness for one day, and she didn't know these people anywhere near as well.

Luckily Sue and Tom didn't seem to mind, or maybe they didn't notice. "Come in. Come in," Sue gushed, as she ushered Sasha up the path, leaving Tom to escort Fran. "Welcome to your new home."

Her words made Sasha shudder. But she didn't want her fear to show so she swallowed hard and stepped through the front door as calmly as she could.

The inside of the house was even neater than the outside. Everything was spotlessly clean, and it smelt of polish and lemon air freshener. Sasha wondered if it was always like this, or whether Sue had tidied up especially for her visit.

Sue took them on a rapid tour of the downstairs. "This is the living room."

"Lovely," said Fran.

"And this is the kitchen."

"Lovely," said Fran. She looked pointedly at Sasha, obviously hoping she would say something.

Sasha didn't. She was too busy taking in the details of the clinically neat room. She much preferred the cosy, untidy kitchen at Kingfishers, but she didn't want to say so in case her voice trembled and gave away how scared she was.

They all trooped up the stairs and followed Sue along the landing. She stopped outside one of the doors and swung it open. Then she smiled at Sasha and waved her through. "This is your room," she announced.

Sasha's fear rose to new heights as she stepped inside. *Your room*. That sounded so final, so settled, as if there was nothing on earth that could change that now.

The room was large and airy and quite attractive, provided you liked pink. Sasha didn't – she'd grown out of that when she was six. But she approved of the TV in one corner – at least she'd be able to escape up here and watch by herself.

"It's lovely," said Fran, predictable as always.

Tom walked over to the smart glass and chrome desk that stood next to the chest of drawers. "We thought you'd need this for your homework. Your new school has a reputation for setting lots of it."

Homework. School. This was getting worse by the minute. Sasha didn't want to sit on her own at a cold, clinical desk while she struggled with work she couldn't do. She wanted to be at the untidy kitchen table at Kingfishers with Beth there to help and encourage her.

She sunk down onto the pink bed, trying to look as if she was testing it for comfort. A huge, aching hole had opened up inside her. This place didn't feel like home, and she was sure it never would.

Lunch didn't improve the situation. They ate at a dining table with a clear glass top, just like the desk. Sue and Tom obviously liked it, but Sasha found it disconcerting to be able to see her feet through a piece of furniture.

Sue beamed as she put a plate down in front of Sasha. "I've made lasagne," she announced. "Beth said it was one of your favourites."

And Dawn's. Had she talked to Beth and Joe yet? And if she had, what had they said? But there was no point in worrying about that now. It was totally out of Sasha's control. So she pushed the thoughts away and tried to concentrate on her food.

She gave Sue full marks for trying but only 2 out of 10 for cooking ability. The lasagne was edible, but the pasta was soggy and the sauce lacked Beth's flair with herbs and spices. The shop-bought cake that followed it tasted over-sweet and slightly artificial. Eating it made Sasha's stomach feel uneasy. Or was that an effect of the growing homesickness inside her?

After lunch, they all went for a walk. Sasha was glad to get out of the unfamiliar house, but she was amazed at how much noise there was. Wherever they went, they could hear the drone of traffic and the roar of planes overhead as they came in to land at the nearby airport. Sue and Tom didn't seem to notice it, but Sasha longed for the peace of the countryside and the gentle sounds of horses.

Tom pointed out the local landmarks as they meandered along the city streets. The leisure centre looked quite welcoming with its huge glass windows that let them see the people swimming inside. But the sight of the huge comprehensive school sent a shiver down Sasha's spine. It was too easy to imagine feeling lost and alone in there.

They crossed a busy road and walked through a park with neatly trimmed hedges and a pond with some bored-looking ducks. Sasha noticed that the sign at the entrance only said "no cycling". That was hardly surprising. It didn't need to say "no horses" because there weren't any horses here to keep out.

Their outing ended at the mall – the perfect place for Sue to indulge her love of shopping. She insisted on buying Sasha a frilly, flouncy skirt that she didn't want. "It makes you look so feminine," she cooed, as she thrust the carrier bag into Sasha's arms.

Sasha took it unwillingly, very aware that Beth would never have forced her to have clothes she didn't like. "I'm more comfortable in jeans."

"You can't wear them all the time," said Tom. "You'll have to wear a skirt to school."

School again. He seemed obsessed with it. Did he have dreams of her winning prizes and passing exams? Maybe he imagined her growing up to be his daughter, the doctor. Or his daughter, the business woman. If so, he was going to be very disappointed.

That wasn't just because of the problems she had at school. It was because Sasha didn't want to be his daughter at all or Sue's. The only people she wanted to be her new mum and dad were Beth and Joe.

Chapter 26

Sasha was pleased when Fran declared it was time to leave. But her future foster parents looked disappointed.

"Bye for now," called Sue, as they waved goodbye.

"See you Tuesday," added Tom.

Tuesday. The word sent a shiver down Sasha's spine. That was only two days away.

Fran drove in silence for a few minutes. Then she said, "Sue and Tom are lovely, aren't they?"

Sasha shrugged. "They're okay, I suppose," she agreed reluctantly. "But I think they want to change me – to make me into their ideal daughter instead of letting me be myself."

"I'm sure you're imagining that. I've been completely straight with them about what you're like."

"But Sue wants me to wear a skirt, and Tom keeps on about school."

Fran sighed. "There's nothing wrong with that – it's what caring parents do. Anyway, it might do you good to change a bit. This horse obsession has got completely out of hand. It isn't helping anyone."

"It helps me," snapped Sasha. Then she lapsed into a sulky silence that Fran filled by turning on the radio. The sound of violins filled the car while Sasha stared out of the window, watching the scenery whiz past without really seeing it. She tried to daydream about riding Meteor, but her mind kept running over the events of the day and her worries about the move.

As they drove up to Kingfishers, Sasha was disappointed to see that Dawn's red car wasn't there. She must have already gone back to college. Had she kept her promise and talked to Joe and Beth? And what had happened if she had?

"How was the visit?" asked Joe, as she climbed out of the car.

Sasha gave a non-committal shrug that hid the turmoil she felt inside. "Okay," she said, without enthusiasm.

Fran came in for a coffee as usual but she stood up as soon as she'd drained her cup. "I'd better be off. It's getting late."

"Please stay a little longer," said Beth. "Dawn had a long chat with us earlier, and now Joe and I would like to talk to you."

Sasha's hopes soared. Dawn must have succeeded. They must be going to say that she didn't have to move – that she could stay here forever. She settled back in her seat, ready to listen to the words she'd longed to hear for so long.

But Beth had other ideas. She handed Sasha an apple and said, "Go and give this to Meteor. We'll call you when we've finished."

It was a gentle order, but an order all the same. Whatever was going to be said in the kitchen was not supposed to be for her ears. That was so unfair. It was her life they were discussing. She should be allowed to hear what they were saying. But this was not the right moment to annoy Beth by arguing, so, very reluctantly, she did as she was told.

She was halfway to Meteor's field when she noticed that the kitchen window was open. She stood still for a moment, torn between her desire to see the bay horse and her need to find out what Joe and Beth were saying about her. Then her curiosity overcame everything else, and she tiptoed back towards the house.

She bent low so she couldn't be seen from inside and crept into position under the window. As soon as she was there, she realised that she'd guessed right. She could hear everything that was being said in the kitchen. So she made herself as comfortable as she could and settled down to listen.

The first voice she heard was Joe's. "We're worried about this move. It all seems to be happening so fast."

"Sasha's being rushed," added Beth. "She hasn't had time to get used to the idea."

"Time is something we haven't got," said Fran. "She only came here on a temporary basis because there was an emergency. We agreed that I'd move her again as soon as I could. Or have you changed your minds about that?"

Sasha held her breath, hardly daring to listen to the answer.

"We have a bit," said Joe.

A bit, thought Sasha. *What does that mean?*

Then Beth explained. "We've talked it over at length with Dawn, and we've decided we're willing to keep her a bit longer – long enough to give her more time to get to know Sue and Tom."

Sasha could hardly believe what she was hearing. *That's wrong. That's not what I want.*

"I don't think time will help," said Fran. "Sasha's big problem seems to be leaving the horses and staying longer will just make that worse."

"Unless you used the extra time to find her a different placement," Joe suggested. "One where she can still ride."

"You must be joking." Fran's exasperation showed in her voice. "I'm not in a position to pick and choose. It's almost impossible to find someone to take a twelve year old, especially one with such a troubled background."

"But you did the ad," said Beth.

"And we got one reply. Sue and Tom are the only people in the country willing to take Sasha, and they're too good to let go. If we start changing the arrangements now, they may back out completely. Sasha's not the only girl they inquired about. They'd have no trouble finding someone else if they can't have her."

"So our offer doesn't make any difference," said Beth.

"No. But I know Sasha is very happy here. I'm willing to let her stay here permanently if you'll take her."

Sasha held her breath again, willing them to say "yes".

"We've thought about that really hard," said Beth. "And Dawn's tried to persuade us too. But we can't make that commitment. Not yet. She's still too emotionally frozen – just like Zack."

Sasha was shocked. Frozen! Her! Surely that wasn't true.

But Joe agreed. "Although she looks as if she's settled, she still hides her feelings. She never cries. And she won't let us close to her."

"But I saw Beth hug her this morning," said Fran. "Wasn't that progress?"

"I hoped so too, but it wasn't. I might as well have been hugging a plank of wood. She was so stiff and unresponsive."

The next voice was Joe's. "We've already failed disastrously with one emotionally frozen child, and we're not going to risk doing it with another. We can't take her permanently unless there's some sign she's going to improve."

"Can't you give us more time?" Beth asked.

Fran sighed. "I can't delay the move while you wait for something that might never happen. Sue and Tom are willing to take her now, just as she is with no strings attached. This might be the last chance Sasha ever gets to have a new family. I can't put that at risk."

There was a long pause. Sasha imagined Joe and Beth looking at each other, wondering if they'd made the right decision.

Then Joe broke the silence. "We're really sorry. We'll have to let her go."

"We'll see you on Tuesday," said Beth. "I'll make sure she's packed and as ready as she can be."

Sasha slumped in her hiding place, her hopes shattered beyond repair. Then the sound of chairs scraping across the floor made her realise the adults inside were standing up. Any minute now, they'd come out and discover what she'd been doing. So she scurried out of sight and raced over to Meteor's field before she was caught.

The bay horse whinnied and cantered over to the fence when he saw her. Then he nuzzled her hand, trying to grab the apple she was still holding. She held it out and let him crunch it while the terrible truth sank in.

All this time she'd been searching for the hidden reason why Joe and Beth wouldn't let her stay. And now she knew. It wasn't Dawn or Jennifer or anyone else.

She was the problem. She'd had too many moves and too many betrayals. She'd lost the ability to trust anyone, and there was nothing she could do to get that back.

Chapter 27

Sasha went through the rest of the day on autopilot, unable to think of anything other than the conversation she had overheard. For a fleeting moment, she wondered if she could force herself to be different — to open up to Joe and Beth. Then she remembered that hug and realised that she couldn't. Her resistance, her fear and her lack of trust were too ingrained. She couldn't fight them or pretend they weren't there.

Her last hope was gone now, leaving her hollow and empty. But it wasn't until the middle of the night that, alone in the darkness of her bedroom, she let herself cry. Even those silent tears didn't help. They were just proof that Joe and Beth were right. She couldn't share her emotions with other people, not even them.

The next morning, she got up as soon as it was light. She was certain now that this was her last full day at Kingfishers, and she was determined not to waste a single minute. So she left a note for Beth on the kitchen table, fed Meteor and then led him out of his field. She needed to think, and the best place to do that was on one of their walks.

Sasha and the bay horse ambled side by side down the bridle path to the river. The kingfisher was there again, searching for breakfast, and the morning sun made dancing shadows on the surface of the water.

She sat down on a fallen tree and told Meteor everything. About Sue and Tom and the new house she didn't want to live in. About how much she wanted to stay at Kingfishers and about it being her fault that they would soon be parted forever.

The bay horse sighed and leaned his head on her shoulder as she spoke. His warm breath and steady breathing helped to calm her. But they also highlighted the unfairness of the situation. Meteor was the only one who really listened to her, and he was powerless to change anything.

When she finally went back to the house, she was pleased to find Beth and Joe weren't trying to pretend this was an ordinary day. Instead they seemed determined to make it as special as they could. Beth had even made pancakes for breakfast because she knew Sasha loved them.

"No lessons this morning," she announced when Sasha had finished scraping the last traces of maple syrup from her plate. "Do you want me to pack for you so you can spend as much time as possible with the horses?"

Packing! Sasha had moved so many times that she knew it had to be done. But she couldn't bear the thought of putting all her things in black sacks again. "It would be great if you did it."

Beth grinned. "Okay. Now get outside and start enjoying yourself."

"I thought you might try lungeing Meteor this morning," said Joe.

"Me!" cried Sasha. She'd spent hours watching Joe lunge the horses he was training, and she'd always assumed that he would be the first person to try it with Meteor.

"Yes, you," said Joe. "You've done all the work to get him this far so it's only fair that you tackle the next step with him. And you know what you're doing – you've managed fine when you've lunged Pumpkin."

Sasha was thrilled. For a moment, she imagined herself standing in the middle of the sand school with the bay horse trotting obediently around her in a circle. But there was something else she dreamed of more than that.

"Can I ride him instead? I won't have another chance after today."

"I know you won't," said Joe with a sympathetic smile. "But Meteor's not ready for riding yet. I'm happy for you to be the first person to lunge him, but I'm not risking you being the first person to get on his back."

Sasha fought back the urge to argue. She could tell from the tone of Joe's voice that it would be pointless, and an angry outburst now would gain nothing. But it had been worth asking anyway, even though it didn't work. She would never have forgiven herself if she hadn't tried.

Half an hour later, she clipped the lunge rein onto Meteor's headcollar and led him into the middle of the sand school. Then she picked up the lunge whip Joe had left on the ground for her. The horse snorted in alarm and stepped away from it. He'd obviously met whips before and had bad memories of them.

"It's okay," soothed Sasha. "I'm not going to hurt you. It's just for signalling – that's all." She reached out and touched his shoulder gently with the end of the whip. Meteor flinched, but didn't move. Then, equally gently, she slid the end of the whip along his back and down his legs, getting him used to the strange feeling and helping him learn that whips didn't always mean pain. After a few minutes, his initial fears had disappeared so much that he stayed totally calm and relaxed while she stroked him all over his body with the whip.

"Good girl," said Joe, who was watching from the fence. "You handled that well."

Confident the horse was ready for the next step, Sasha held the lunge rein in one hand and the whip in the other and backed away from him. “Walk on,” she called.

Meteor did as he was told. But he didn’t walk round in a circle like she’d expected. Instead, he turned and walked up to her. That took her by surprise. Pumpkin had never done that.

“He doesn’t understand what you want,” said Joe. “He’s so used to walking beside you that he’s confused by you asking him to walk away.”

“So what do I do?”

“You concentrate on lungeing him properly. Keep your eyes on his saddle area and make a triangle with the rein, the whip and his body. I’ll go beside him for a while to help him get the right idea.”

With Joe’s help, Meteor quickly learned what he was supposed to be doing. Soon he was walking around Sasha in a perfect circle without any tension on the lunge line. And he kept going when Joe left him alone and went back to the fence.

Sasha successfully stopped and started Meteor a few times. Then she asked him to trot, and the bay horse obediently changed pace. The longer she worked him, the better he became, and he was just as good when she asked him to circle in the other direction.

“Well done,” said Joe. “He’s so calm you’d think he’d been doing it for years. Now we’ll call that a day. He’s worked hard.”

Sasha brought Meteor to a halt. Then she went over and made a fuss of him. "You are a clever boy," she said.

"There's no doubt about that," said Joe, as he joined her. He tickled the horse's withers and added, "He'll fetch a good price in a few months' time."

Sasha stared at him in horror. "You mean you're going to sell him."

"Of course we are. That's what we do for a living. We buy horses, we train them and then we sell them again."

"But Beth said you keep the useful ones, and Meteor's going to be useful. I'm sure he is."

Joe shook his head. "I don't think he'll be useful enough for us. We only keep the ones that are a bit special, like Calypso with his talent for jumping."

Sasha felt utterly miserable as she led Meteor into his field. He was just like her – damaged by too many moves and too many bad experiences. And just like her, he'd found a safe haven at Kingfishers, somewhere he could be himself without pretending. They were both happy here together, and now it looked as if both of them would have to leave.

She unbuckled the headcollar and turned Meteor loose. He nuzzled her hand briefly. Then he wandered away and started to graze. He looked so calm and relaxed, completely unaware that he couldn't stay here forever.

Sasha knew her own fate was sealed. But at least she knew why she was leaving and where she was going. It would be far worse for Meteor. When the time came for him to leave, he would just be loaded into a horsebox with no explanation and driven away to live with strangers.

She shuddered as she remembered how terrified he'd been when he arrived. Moving him again risked re-awakening all his old fears and undoing all the progress he had made at Kingfishers. And if he went back to his old ways, he could end up being moved from home to home again or, worse still, he might be put down.

Sasha couldn't bear to let that happen. She had to do something to save him. But what? All her plans to make Joe and Beth keep *her* had failed completely. Could she do better for Meteor? And could she do it fast enough? After tomorrow, there would be no way she could help him. She needed to know he was safe before she left.

She walked slowly back to the house for lunch, still struggling to think of a way to solve the problem. She went on thinking all the time she was munching her tuna and sweetcorn sandwiches. It was only as she swallowed the last mouthful that the idea came. Suppose she rode Meteor. Would that help her discover a reason why he was special enough to stay?

She glanced furtively across the table at Joe. She'd meant what she said after that first disastrous lesson when she'd promised to always do what he told her. And she knew only too well that he had told her not to ride the bay horse. But he was wrong before when he thought it was soon to put a headcollar on him. Perhaps he was wrong again now.

She hoped he was, because her idea had already turned into a plan. She had nothing left to lose now so, promise or no promise, she was determined to ride Meteor. And she had to do it this afternoon. It was the last chance she would ever have.

Chapter 28

Sasha gulped down her cup of tea and slipped out of the kitchen while Joe and Beth were still drinking theirs. It would be a few minutes before they went outside too – just enough time to put the first stage of her plan into action.

She headed straight for the tack room and found Meteor's tack. His bridle was well worn, but it didn't look too bad. The leather was soft and supple from where she'd oiled it on the day she'd made such a mess in the tack room. His saddle was much worse. It was old and battered with a split across the back. The leather was dry and brittle from years of neglect and some of the stitching had rotted away. But it was all she had. It would have to do.

She hung the bridle over her shoulder, put her riding hat on her head and picked up the saddle. Then she peeped out of the tack room door to see if there was any sign of Joe or Beth. There wasn't. The coast was clear provided she was quick.

She ran out of the far end of the yard and set off along the path that led to the river. But before she'd gone halfway, she turned left into a field bounded by a hedge that hid it from the rest of the farm. There was no chance of Beth and Joe noticing what she was doing in here.

She walked beside the hedge until she found a large enough gap between the bottom branches to make a perfect hiding place. She slid the saddle into it, being careful to stand it on its front edge. Although it was already in a state, she didn't want it getting any more damage. Then she slid the bridle and her hat in beside it and pulled some dead branches across the gap to hide them all from view.

She stepped back and surveyed her handiwork. The saddle was completely hidden. There was no possibility that anyone would discover it before she came back. Stage one of her plan had gone smoothly. Now it was time for stage two.

She ran swiftly back the way she had come, dived into the tack room and grabbed Meteor's headcollar. But, as she stepped out into the yard again, she met Joe coming in the opposite direction.

"Do you want to ride Pumpkin?" he asked. "I can put some jumps up for you if you like."

The idea was so tempting that it was hard to resist. But that would mean abandoning her plan, and she wasn't prepared to do that. "I'd love to," she said. "But I promised Meteor I'd take him for a walk."

"Another one?" said Joe. "He's certainly getting lots of attention today."

"There's nothing wrong with that," snapped Sasha, suddenly defensive. He'd spoil everything if he stopped her taking Meteor out.

Joe held up his hands in apology. "I wasn't criticising – honestly I wasn't. You spend as much time with him as you like. Store up some happy memories to take with you."

Sasha hurried off, glad to get away before he asked any questions about the walk she was planning. She was already uneasy about breaking her promise to him and didn't want to have to lie to him as well.

Meteor whinnied with pleasure when he saw her and trotted over to the gate, apparently happy to be caught again. She buckled on his headcollar and led him towards the river. As they walked side by side, she explained her plan. She wasn't sure he understood, but talking about it did her good anyway. It kept her calm and helped her work out the details of what she was about to do.

When they reached the field, she glanced along the hedge and had a sudden moment of panic. What if she'd hidden his saddle and bridle so well that even she couldn't find them again? Then she recognised the dead branches she'd used to hide everything from view, and she relaxed.

It didn't take Sasha long to drag the branches away and pull the saddle and bridle out onto the grass. Meteor snorted and pulled away when he saw them. Sasha held onto his rope, but let him retreat to a place where he felt safer. Then she waited patiently without trying to force him to do anything.

Eventually the horse's curiosity got the better of him. He stepped forward gingerly and stretched out his neck to sniff the objects on the ground. Sasha gave him as much time as he needed to explore them and discover they didn't move. There was no rush – she had all afternoon. So she waited until she was sure he was completely relaxed before she bent down and picked up the bridle.

This time Meteor didn't flinch. Instead, he stayed calm with his head low. "Good boy," said Sasha, as she held out the bridle for him to sniff again. Then she took the reins in her right hand and gently slipped them over his head.

It must have been a long time since anyone did that to the bay horse, but he didn't seem to mind. Confident that he would stand beside her, she took off his headcollar and hung it over her shoulder. Then she lifted the bridle, ready to put it on. Meteor opened his mouth easily for the bit and waited patiently while she slid the headpiece over his ears and fastened the throatlash and noseband.

Sasha pulled his long, black forelock from under the browband and stepped back to admire her work. He looked good with his bridle on. It complemented the shape of his face beautifully and made her excited about the ride ahead.

She looped her arm through the reins and turned her attention to the saddle. It was in an even worse state than she remembered, and she regretted not bringing a numnah to go between his back and the stiff leather. But it was too late to go and get one now without being seen.

"Sorry," she said, as she put the saddle well forward on Meteor's withers and slid it back into the right position. He flicked his ears back as he felt the pressure of it on his back. Then he relaxed again.

Sasha ducked under his head and went round to the other side of the saddle to sort out the girth. Luckily that was one of those cloth ones with lots of stitching. It was filthy, but it was still soft and flexible. Which was more than could be said for the girth straps. They were made of leather and as dry and stiff as the rest of the saddle. Worse still, one of the holes had a split running through it that ran almost right across the strap. Sasha carefully moved the girth onto a higher hole. She didn't want the strap to break while she was riding.

She went back to Meteor's left side, reached underneath him and grabbed the girth. His ears went back again as he felt it touch his belly. Sasha paused to give him time to get used to it and didn't try to do up the girth until she was sure he was happy. Then she pulled it tight gradually, tugging the buckles up the unwieldy straps one hole at a time. Luckily there were no splits in them on this side.

"Almost ready," she said, as she stroked his shoulder. She hung the headcollar on the hedge, pulled her hat from its hiding place and pushed it onto her head. Then she pulled down the stirrups, one at a time. She was relieved to find that they moved easily. The stirrup leathers were much less stiff than the rest of the saddle. Sometime in the past, they must have been well oiled – maybe too well. The leather was so soft it had stretched thin with years of use.

Sasha felt a nervous flutter in her stomach as she took hold of the reins. Suppose Joe was right. Suppose Meteor wasn't ready to ride yet. But there would never be another chance – not for her. If she wanted to ride Meteor, she had to do it now.

Chapter 29

Sasha gave Meteor's neck one more stroke. Then she took a deep breath, put her foot in the stirrup and swung herself into the saddle. She landed as gently as she could, but Meteor still raised his head anxiously when he felt her weight on his back.

"Steady, boy," she said, reaching down with one hand to scratch his withers. She knew he loved that – it always made him relax and today was no exception.

As soon as he was calm again, she quickly adjusted her stirrups. Then she took more contact on the reins and gently nudged his sides with her legs. He walked forward, calmly and obediently. His stride was longer than Pumpkin's and very comfortable.

Halfway across the field, she decided she should check that she had some brakes. She pushed her weight down in the saddle and resisted the forward motion with her hands, just like Joe had told her. Meteor didn't stop immediately – she had to pull the reins gently to help him understand what she wanted. But the next time she tried, he stopped much quicker and he kept improving. After a few goes, she found she only had to think the word "*stop*" and shift her weight slightly in the saddle to bring him to a halt.

Pumpkin had never been as responsive as this. It was almost as if he could read her mind. That thought filled her with confidence and tempted her to be more ambitious. Could she use the slightest of signals to get him to do other things as well?

In her head, she matched her thoughts to the rhythm of his walk: 1 2 3 4, 1 2 3 4. Then she changed the rhythm to 1 2, 1 2 and pressed her legs lightly against his sides. To her delight, Meteor changed pace to a steady trot that matched the beats in her head. His long legs covered the ground so smoothly that his trot was much less bouncy than Pumpkin's, and Sasha found she didn't need to rise up and down as fast as she usually did.

She turned him onto a large circle and trotted right round in both directions. Then she tried some transitions, changing from trot to walk and back again. Once again, Meteor responded to the slightest signals so she tried being more ambitious. Soon he was switching from trot to halt and halt to trot just as willingly. Sasha was thrilled. She'd never managed to do that before with Pumpkin.

But there was still one big test left. Would thinking the change work with that too? She switched the rhythm in her mind to 1 2 3, 1 2 3 and breathed out gently. Equally gently, Meteor switched pace to a steady canter without speeding up. It was incredibly comfortable – just like a rocking horse. Sasha had no problem keeping her seat in the saddle as her body moved in time with his. She and Meteor were perfectly in tune – matching each other without effort.

This was magic. Better than her wildest dreams. He really was the perfect horse – willing, skilful and totally amazing. Surely Joe and Beth would agree to keep him when they saw how special he was. Perhaps she should go and show them now.

Then she glanced at the open gate at the top of the field – the gate that led to Buckberry Ridge. There was still plenty of time before she had to take Meteor back – time to fulfil one last dream.

She cantered over to the gateway, slowed to a trot to go through it and then asked Meteor to canter again. The long grassy track lay ahead of them like a racetrack. Sasha could feel Meteor's excitement as she urged him into a gallop. She leaned forward, balancing her weight perfectly in the stirrups as his pounding hooves carried her faster and faster across the smooth turf. This was fantastic – far better than she had imagined.

Suddenly, without any warning, the right stirrup leather snapped. The iron vanished from under her foot, throwing her completely off balance. She pitched sideways and lost contact with the saddle. For a second, she seemed to hang there, horribly aware there was no longer a horse underneath her. Then she hurtled downwards and crashed onto the ground.

It was a bad fall at full speed. But she rolled as she landed, which helped lessen the force of the impact. When she finally stopped moving, she lay on her back, scared and shaken, and looked around for Meteor. What if he hadn't stopped? What if he'd had an accident himself?

She was relieved to see him standing a few metres away, watching her anxiously. "Don't worry," she said, trying to reassure herself as much as him. "It was an accident. It wasn't your fault." A little voice at the back of her mind suggested that it might have been hers, but she decided to ignore it.

She closed her eyes and did a mental check of her body to see if she was hurt. Her head seemed all right and she could twiddle her fingers and toes. Her arms seemed okay too and so was her right leg. But her left ankle was definitely not happy.

She opened her eyes again and discovered than Meteor had come over to her while she wasn't looking. He put his head down close to hers and whickered gently, wafting warm breath over her face.

Sasha struggled into a sitting position and tried to stand up. But as soon as she put some weight on her left foot, a searing pain shot through her ankle. She bit her lip hard, forcing herself not to scream. She didn't want to scare Meteor.

She lay back onto the ground and waited for the pain to ease. As soon as it was bearable, she rolled over and managed to get up on her hands and knees. "Stand still," she told Meteor and started to crawl along his left side. It wasn't easy. Although she kept her injured foot off the ground, she couldn't keep it completely still. And every time it moved, she felt another twinge of pain.

Meteor behaved perfectly, doing exactly as he was told. He watched her strange behaviour with curiosity. But he didn't move at all.

At last, she reached her target – the place where the one remaining stirrup dangled from his saddle. Biting her lip against the pain, she forced herself to kneel. Then she put one hand on his foreleg to balance herself and reached up with the other to try to grab the one remaining stirrup. She failed once. Twice. But on the third try, her fingers closed on the cold metal.

So far, so good. Now she just had to stand up. She shifted her weight onto her left knee while she moved her right leg so that her foot was flat on the ground ready to carry her. Then she pulled hard on the stirrup and tried to heave herself up. It nearly worked. But at the last minute, she wobbled slightly and instinctively put her left leg down to steady herself. This time the pain was excruciating, and Sasha did the only thing she could. She screamed.

Meteor jumped sideways in alarm, taking the stirrup with him. Sasha managed to let go of it before it pulled her over. But without it, she had no way to keep her balance. She fell to the ground again, the pain so bad that it made her feel sick.

The bay horse watched her with wild, frightened eyes. He snorted and backed away, his body tense and ready for action.

"Come here, Meteor," she pleaded. "I need you."

But Meteor didn't come. Instead he gave another loud snort, whirled on the spot and galloped away down the hill. The one lone stirrup banged against his side as he ran.

"No," wailed Sasha as she watched him vanish into the distance. He was her friend. Her trusted companion. He couldn't leave her now.

A wave of despair swept over her. Everyone had abandoned her. First Joe and Beth and now even Meteor. No one loved her. No one cared. She was totally alone, and she didn't know what to do. Tears poured down her face and, for the first time for years, she howled out loud. There was no need to cry silently now because there was no one close enough to hear.

Chapter 30

Sasha lay on the grass and cried until there were no tears left. But it didn't help. When she eventually stopped, her despair was still there and so was a growing sense of panic.

She shivered despite the sunshine. The ground was wet from the recent rain, and the dampness was seeping through her clothes, chilling her body and adding to her misery. It would be awful to be out here all night, alone in the cold and the dark.

She wondered how long it would be before Joe and Beth realised she was missing. Even when they did, there were so many places she could be that it might be hours or even days before they thought of looking for her up here.

Suddenly she heard a voice calling her name. She sat up and looked around, but she couldn't see anyone.

The voice came again, deep and strong. It was Joe. "Sasha! Where are you?"

"I'm here," she shouted as loudly as she could. She hoped desperately that he could hear her. It would be dreadful if he missed her when he'd come so close.

Then she saw the most welcome sight in the world. It was Joe leading Meteor. Or she thought it was. It was only as they came closer that she realised she was wrong. Meteor was in front. He was leading Joe. The bay horse hadn't abandoned her after all. He'd gone to fetch help, and now he was showing Joe where she was.

"I'm here," Sasha shouted again, waving both her hands in her air.

To her relief, Joe spotted her and waved back. Then he ran towards her with Meteor trotting eagerly by his side. Sasha quickly wiped her face with her sleeve. She didn't want him seeing any trace of the tears she'd shed.

As soon as he reached her, Joe dropped onto his knees beside her. "Are you hurt?" he asked, his face full of concern.

"It's my ankle. I can't put any weight on it at all."

Meteor looked worried too. He dropped his head and nuzzled her shoulder. Sasha reached up and stroked his face. "Thanks for coming back," she whispered. Then she turned to Joe and said, "I'm sorry. I really am."

"I'm glad about that," Joe said softly. "But I'm not going to make a big deal of it – you've learned your lesson the hard way. And right now, it's more important to get you home." He pulled his mobile phone from his pocket and called Beth. "It's all right. I've found her. She's on Buckberry Ridge, but I think she might have broken her ankle." He listened for a moment, nodding in agreement with what was being said.

Then he put the phone away and spoke to Sasha. "Beth's bringing the Land Rover to fetch you. But she can't drive up to here. We'll have to meet her down in the field." He pointed back the way he had come – the same route Sasha and Meteor had galloped along before the accident.

"But I can't walk," said Sasha.

"Don't worry," said Joe. "I can carry you."

Sasha went rigid with fear. She couldn't bear the thought of Joe lifting her up in his arms. Being carried wouldn't feel like rescue. It would feel like being trapped.

Meteor nudged her shoulder again, as if he was trying to attract her attention. And that made her realise there was another solution. "I could ride Meteor," she said. "You'll just have to help me get on." That would involve being close too, but at least it wouldn't last for so long.

Joe looked doubtful. "I'm not sure about that. He's the reason you're hurt in the first place."

"No, he's not," said Sasha. "He was brilliant — the perfect horse. He did everything I asked of him. I only fell off because the stirrup leather snapped."

Joe scratched his head thoughtfully. "I suppose it's worth a try. You should be safe enough if I lead him."

Sasha was sure she'd be safe even if he didn't. But she didn't argue.

"I'll give you a leg-up," Joe continued. "But first you've got to stand on your good leg. Shall I pick you up?"

"No," said Sasha. "I can do it myself. I'm sure I can. I nearly managed it before."

She waited while Joe led Meteor over so he was standing right beside her. When she was sure he was in the best possible position, she rolled onto her hands and knees like she had earlier and moved her good leg so her foot was flat on the ground. Then she grabbed hold of Joe with one hand and Meteor's stirrup with the other and pulled herself upright.

She stiffened instinctively as Joe put his arm out to steady her. But he only kept it there for an instant. Then she was standing on her right leg, holding Meteor's saddle for balance. She kept her other leg off the ground, trying to move her injured ankle as little as possible.

"Ready," said Joe. He took hold of her left leg just below the knee and said, "One, two, three, go." On the last word, he lifted her with all his strength and Sasha flew upwards, almost blinded with pain.

She swung her good leg over Meteor's back and landed in the saddle with more force than she'd hoped. She grabbed hold of his mane to steady herself while the agony receded. Then she smiled at Joe and said, "Let's go."

They walked slowly down the hill with Joe in front holding the reins and Sasha perched in the saddle, wincing gently. Each step Meteor took made her ankle hurt more, but it also took her closer to safety.

She breathed a sigh of relief when they reached the waiting Land Rover. Her ordeal was finally over, and her despair had vanished too. None of them had abandoned her. Joe, Beth and Meteor all cared enough to save her.

She slid down from the saddle and landed successfully on her good leg. Then, with Beth hovering on one side and Joe on the other, she hopped over to the Land Rover, trying to hold on to them as little as possible.

"Hospital for you, young lady," Beth declared. She drove down to the house and waited while Joe untacked Meteor and turned him out. As soon as he'd finished, he jumped into the front passenger seat, and they all set off for town.

Sasha sank back against the well-worn upholstery, exhausted by the events of the day and the continual pain. She was only vaguely aware that Joe was phoning Fran to let her know what had happened. She knew from experience that foster parents always had to do that. She was officially Social Services responsibility, not theirs.

"Will this mean I can't move tomorrow?" she asked when the call was over. She didn't mind how much her injury hurt if it gave her more time at Kingfishers.

To her disappointment, Joe shook his head. "Fran is sure it won't."

So that was it – her last chance gone. But maybe there was still hope for Meteor. Maybe there was still a chance she could save him from moving again now she knew how fantastic he was to ride.

Sasha decided not to try to talk about him during the journey. It was hard to judge the right words when she could only see the back of Joe and Beth's heads instead of their faces. And it was difficult to talk over the rumble of the engine and the various rattles and squeaks that gave the old Land Rover its character.

Luckily the long wait at the Accident and Emergency Department provided the opportunity she needed. Sasha chose her opening words with care. "I wish you'd seen me riding Meteor."

"I wish I had too," said Joe. "Then I could have told you to get off, and we wouldn't all be sitting here now."

"But if you'd seen me, you'd have realised what a fantastic horse he is. He did everything I wanted almost before I asked him. It was as if he could read my mind."

Beth looked up from the magazine she was reading and frowned. "What do you mean by that?"

"I just thought what I wanted him to do, and he did it. So when I wanted to go from a trot to a canter, I changed the rhythm in my head from 1 2, 1 2 to 1 2 3, 1 2 3 and he changed pace."

"And did that work when you slowed down too?" asked Beth.

"Yes," said Sasha, delighted to see she was so interested. "He was really amazing."

"He was pretty amazing when he came to fetch us," said Joe. "He galloped into the yard and screeched to a halt. Then he kept trotting up to us and trotting away again before we could catch him. It took us a while to realise he wanted us to follow him."

Beth shook her head in disbelief. "I've only ever seen animals behave like that in movies. I didn't think horses ever did that in real life."

Sasha looked from one of them to the other. "So is he amazing enough for you to keep? You said you keep the horses that are special."

There was a long pause while Joe and Beth looked at each other. "I'm not sure," Beth said eventually.

"We'll have to think about it," added Joe.

That wasn't the reply that Sasha wanted. She was just opening her mouth to argue when the conversation was cut short by the arrival of a nurse who whisked her away in a wheelchair to have an X-ray.

Sasha was lucky. Her ankle wasn't broken. It was just badly sprained. She felt much better by the time the nurse had bandaged it tightly and dosed her up with strong painkillers. She was able to walk back to the car with the help of a stick, and the doctor reckoned she wouldn't even need that by the morning.

Unfortunately the painkillers made her feel woozy. That made talking so difficult that she was forced to give up trying to persuade Joe and Beth to keep Meteor. By the time she went to bed, she felt absolutely dismal. All she'd managed to prise out of them was that promise to "think about it". And she knew from experience that adults thinking about things usually ended up with them saying "no".

Chapter 31

Thanks to the painkillers, Sasha spent the night in a deep, dreamless sleep. She awoke to find sunlight streaming through her window, illuminating the pile of bulging black sacks that held everything she possessed. Her last morning at Kingfishers had finally arrived.

She stood up cautiously and found she could tolerate a little weight on her bad leg now, provided it didn't stay there for long. So she limped downstairs for her last breakfast. Beth was cooking again, and the kitchen was filled with the delicious smell of bacon. Normally that would make Sasha feel hungry, but it didn't today. She was too miserable and scared to eat.

"You're looking better," said Joe, as he pulled out her chair to make it easier for her to sit down. He waited until she was settled, then he pushed it back in again so she could reach the table easily.

Beth handed Sasha a brightly wrapped parcel. "We got you this. It's a good-luck present to remember us by."

Sasha didn't want a goodbye present. She wanted to stay. But a parcel was exciting all the same. She pulled off the paper and found another photo album, almost the same as the one from Sue and Tom. But this one was much better. As she turned the pages, she saw picture after picture of Kingfishers. All the horses were there, even Bambi who'd been sold, and there were more of Meteor than of any of the others.

"Thanks," said Sasha, hugging the album to her chest. "It's great."

"I'm glad you're pleased," said Beth. She reached out as if she was going to put an arm round Sasha's shoulder. Then she had second thoughts and stopped.

The pictures reminded Sasha of the unfinished conversation from yesterday. She hadn't completed her task. Meteor's future was still as uncertain as her own. "Have you thought about Meteor?" she asked. "You promised you would."

Joe shook his head. "It's too early to decide. We'll have to wait and see how he turns out."

"But he's got to stay here – he must." The words poured out of her in a torrent. "Don't you understand? He's had too many moves in his life – too many fresh starts with strangers who've let him down. He can't cope with another one – not now, not when he's finally learning to trust again." She paused for breath, knowing only too well that everything she'd said applied to her as much as Meteor.

Then she spoke again – begging, pleading. "I've got to go. I know that. I promise I'll leave without making a fuss, and I promise I'll do my best to fit in with Sue and Tom. But please, please, promise me that Meteor can stay. I don't want him to lose all the progress he's made. I don't want him to go back to how he was." She paused again, gathering the courage to reveal the whole truth. Then she added quietly, "I love him too much to let that happen."

Joe and Beth said nothing for a moment. It was as if the storm of words from Sasha had left them speechless. Then they glanced at each other and something unspoken seemed to pass between them. They both nodded slightly before they turned back to Sasha.

"I'm impressed," said Joe. "That was a remarkable speech, right from the heart."

"And I think you're right," said Beth. "We should keep Meteor. Not because he's amazing or wonderful – which he is. But because you want it so much that you've put his needs before your own."

Sasha wasn't sure she understood what Beth was talking about. But she didn't care. All that mattered was that Meteor's future was settled. Her own was still precarious but, whatever happened to her, she'd always know that he was safe and happy at Kingfishers.

With the difficult conversation over, Sasha lapsed into silence and concentrated on her breakfast. The bacon and egg went beautifully together, but she could hardly eat them. Her mouth was too dry, and her stomach was tied in nervous knots. She was painfully aware of the kitchen clock ticking away the last minutes of her time at Kingfishers.

She hoped Fran would be late, but she wasn't. For the first time ever, the social worker turned up early. "I'm dying for a coffee," she said, as she came into the kitchen.

"I'll put Sasha's things in the car while you're drinking it," said Joe.

"You'd better put this in my rucksack," said Sasha, handing him the album of horse photos. "I've got to say goodbye to Meteor."

"Do you want me to come with you?" he asked. "It's quite a walk."

"I can manage," said Sasha. She didn't want anyone else there, spoiling her final moments with the horse she loved.

She stood up, using the edge of the table to get her balance. Then she limped out of the kitchen, heading for Meteor's field. She'd walked this route so often that she knew every step by heart. It felt so strange knowing that she'd never do it again.

Meteor cantered over to meet her, as he always did. He hung his head over the fence and, as soon as she was close enough, he nuzzled her arm in greeting. Sasha stroked his neck and put her face close to his, breathing in the delightful scent of horse. Then she ran her fingers through his black mane and stroked his soft, brown coat, trying to imprint every detail of this wonderful horse on her brain. She wanted to remember him always, just like this – happy and contented and incredibly beautiful.

She stayed close beside him until she heard Joe calling her back to the house. The car was loaded. Fran was ready. The moment she'd been dreading had finally arrived.

She threw her arms round Meteor's neck and hugged him. "Goodbye," she whispered. "I've got to go. But I'll never forget you. I promise." Then she turned and limped sadly away. Her throat was tight with grief, but she couldn't allow herself to cry – not here, not now, not in front of Joe and Beth and Fran. Even after everything that had happened and everything she knew, she didn't feel safe doing that.

Meteor whinnied after her. She glanced back and saw him, head up and eyes full of anxiety. But she couldn't go back to him now. She had to leave. She had no choice.

He whinnied again and again. There was an edge of desperation to the sound as if he realised she was going forever. Sasha felt desperate too. It was so hard to leave him. But she kept going, limping away from him towards Fran's waiting car.

She was almost there when he stopped calling. She glanced back and saw him trotting away from her across the field. It looked as if he'd given up and decided to leave her too. That made her feel even worse. She wanted this over with as soon as possible so she tried to walk faster, despite her painful ankle.

Suddenly Sasha heard a gasp of surprise from Beth and the sound of pounding hooves behind her. She swung round and saw Meteor galloping towards the fence. What was he doing? If he didn't stop soon, he'd crash into it and hurt himself.

But Meteor had other ideas. As he raced up to the fence, he pushed his powerful back legs against the ground and soared into the air. It was a fantastic jump that took him right over the top rail with space to spare. As soon as he landed, he galloped on, straight towards Fran's car.

For a moment, Sasha thought he was going to jump that too. But he didn't. Instead, he skidded to a halt and turned to face her, blocking her path. Then he stepped forward and nudged her with his nose, pushing her away from the car. There was no doubt now what he was doing. He was trying to stop her leaving.

He loved her. He didn't want her to go. And that knowledge made something inside her melt, releasing all the emotions she'd kept bottled up for so long. For the first time ever, she didn't care who was watching. She buried her face in his mane and cried.

She was sobbing so hard that she didn't hear Beth's footsteps coming up behind her. She just heard Beth whisper, "It's all right," and felt her arms around her.

That hug was the same as the one that had made her go rigid on Sunday morning. But Sasha didn't feel threatened by it now. She felt protected instead. She turned slightly and put her own arm around Beth's waist in response, pulling her closer. And when she looked up, she saw through her tears that Beth was weeping too. But she didn't seem sad – the smile on her face suggested she was happy.

Then Joe was there too, hugging them both and grinning broadly while tears ran down his cheeks. Sasha put her other arm round him and pulled him close too. It felt so right to be touching them both now.

She had no idea how long they stood there – Sasha, Joe, Beth and Meteor all joined together in one group hug. But gradually her sobs died away and she started to smile too. She felt better inside than she had for a very long time.

Fran coughed gently to attract their attention. "I really should be going," she said. "But this horse is in the way."

"No, he's not," said Joe. "He's in exactly the right place. Sometimes it takes a horse to show us what we need to know."

"Which is?" asked Fran.

Joe looked questioningly at Beth. She nodded and hugged Sasha tight. Then she turned to Fran and said, "We've changed our minds. We want Sasha to stay forever."

Sasha could hardly believe her ears. Could this really be happening now, when she'd given up all hope? She looked questioningly at Fran. The social worker controlled her life. Would she say it was too late to cancel the move?

To her relief, Fran beamed with pleasure. "That's fine by me. Provided Sasha still wants to stay."

Sasha nearly jumped up and down in excitement, but she remembered her sprained ankle just in time and forced herself to stand still while she shouted, "I do, I do, I do."

Then she kissed Meteor gently on his forehead. "We'll always be together now," she said. She'd already made sure that he would stay at Kingfishers forever. Now he had done the same for her.

About the Author

Diana Kimpton has always loved horses, and writing about them gives her the perfect excuse to go to the stables when she should be working. Despite all her time-wasting activities, she has written more than 40 books for children, including The Pony-Mad Princess series, as well as two books for adults.

You can find out about Diana's other books at
www.dianakimpton.co.uk

CPSIA information can be obtained
at www.ICGtesting.com
Printed in the USA
FSOW04n1928041016
25742FS